The Fool Stories

Book One

The Adventure Begins

Dr. Jessica Hart
Illustrated by Brian Keeler

Words of Wizdom

International, Inc.
Miami Beach · Florida

Words of Wizdom International, Inc., P.O. Box 403647, Miami Beach, FL 33140
To Order: 1-800-834-7612

Illustrator: Brian Keeler
Text Design: J. Severn, PhD.
Edited by: Leslie Weld
Type Selection: Alexander Kohlrautz
Cover Design: Jonathan Pennell
Manufactured in China

Library of Congress Cataloging-in-Publication Data

Hart, Jessica, 1952-
    The Fool stories / Jessica Hart ; illustrated by Brian Keeler.
        p.   cm.
    Contents: Bk. 1. The adventure begins
    Summary: The Fool, a travelling storyteller, meets people,
animals, and extraterrestrial beings on his journeys and shares his
tales with them.
    ISBN 1-884695-09-4 (v. 1) : $18.95 ($25.50 Can.)
    [1. Storytelling--Fiction.] I. Keeler, Brian, 1953-   ill.
II. Title.
PZ7.H25684Fo   1994
[Fic]--dc20   94-46925
                                                               CIP
                                                               AC

Dedicated To:

Grandma

Contents

**Join Fool and his friends on the
following adventures
in
Book One**

Chapter One

Chapter Three

The Story of Beth and Her Friend From Space

Fool's Journey
Where Fool and Intuit hitch a ride with the Amazing Donald
and his hot air balloon show.

Chapter Four

Frequent Flyer

Fool's Journey
Where Fool and Intuit sneak into the forest, and
Intuit prepares to do battle with an old brown bear.

Chapter Five

Sacred Circle

Fool's Journey
Where Fool is just too tired to go on, and
the old brown bear finds a simple solution.

Chapter One

<u>Grandmother Hattie and The Blankets of White Light</u>

Part I: How Fool Became The Storyteller

Long, long ago, high in the mountains in a land found only in deep restful sleep, nestled the Village of Dreams. On the edge of the village, not too far from the forest and quite close to the ocean, lived a very old and extremely wise woman. Grandmother Hattie. Grandmother Hattie wore dresses of faded cotton and smelled of crushed, dried flowers and frying pork chops. Her hair wisped around her face as lightly as clouds traveling high in a summer sky. Long, silver, and as shiny as minnows flashing in a river, it flowed from her old head, across the floor of the porch, and down two steps to the grass. Sometimes visitors reached out and patted her silky hair. It was common knowledge that touching Grandmother Hattie's hair would bring sweet dreams of flying. She looked frail, but she was alert and strong, and she moved around her little cottage with confidence.

Grandmother Hattie was no ordinary wise woman. No way. Because she was very, very magical, she was very, very special. Time changed around Grandmother Hattie. Big clocks stopped ticking, and the hands on wrist watches went round and round really fast. When children stopped by to chat, hours turned into dandelion puffs and floated away on the breeze.

Even Grandmother Hattie's soft and wrinkled skin held magic for each child who visited. In the eyes of Kitonga, the boy from the dark parts of the forest, her skin seemed as black as night. When Flying Sun, the girl from the plains, looked at her, Grandmother Hattie's skin warmed to cinnamon. Su Lynn, from a place called Asia, beheld a tawny skinned old woman with almond shaped eyes. Aldolpho watched a nonni the color of olives from his father's fields. Nancy, a shy little girl from the country to the North, felt safe with a pale pink grandma sitting peacefully in the sunlight.

Grandmother Hattie had a helper named Fool. It is very good luck, in the Village of Dreams, to be named Fool. Fool is a word that means Silly, and Silly means Blessed. Fool, a thin elf of a boy, always wore soft yellow boots, brown tights and a pair of green shorts with a loose matching shirt that flowed around his body as he moved. A long red feather stuck out of his little green cap. His sparkling eyes were ocean blue, his hair the color of yellow sand, and his skin a suntanned brown. Fool always danced a little when he moved, happy to have the job of helper to Grandmother Hattie.

Each day after school, the children of the Village of Dreams followed the path that led to the magical cottage of Grandmother Hattie. Through the willow grove, past the little duck pond, and around the strawberry patch they hiked, laughing and singing as they went. She would be waiting there on her big front porch, rocking in her old brown chair. Waiting, with a story.

Fool helped by putting plates of warm cookies and large buckets of ice cold coconut juice or limeade on the steps of the porch. As the children helped themselves to treats, Grandmother Hattie smiled and asked about the day at school. Children could talk to Grandmother Hattie about anything that was going on in their lives. She listened carefully, and she cared about what children said. As they talked, Fool made himself useful by pouring more cups of cool drink, or fetching more plates of warm cookies.

When the children settled down, the storytelling began. Of course, because Grandmother Hattie was magical, each child heard the stories in the language of his or her own country. While Grandmother Hattie told rare and wonderful stories, Fool stood quietly behind her, combing her long silver hair with a comb made of seashells. With every

stroke, a few strands would gently tangle in the comb. Fool carefully removed these from the comb and placed them neatly in a grass basket.

Each night when all the visitors had gone home and all the dishes were washed, Grandmother Hattie pulled her chair next to a loom made from the bones of seabirds. In the glow of light from the fireplace she began to weave. Pulling strands of silver hair from the basket, she wove beautiful, glistening blankets. The blankets were very warm, and because they were woven from magical hair, they were also light and shiny. Everyone called them the Blankets of White Light. When the weaving was done, Fool carefully folded the Blankets and put them in the linen closet.

Grandmother Hattie used the Blankets of White Light for a very special purpose. Just outside the Village of Dreams lived a Trickster named Fear. Fear thought it was really funny to see people so afraid that they made mistakes, or got angry, or hurt themselves or their friends. Fear's favorite trick was to sneak around and blow freezing cold breath on the back of a person's neck. Then, "frozen" with Fear, the person would be unable to make good decisions, or to get out of trouble. To help people deal with Trickster Fear, Grandmother Hattie wrapped them in Blankets of White Light. Warmed by the Blankets, it was easy for people to see that Fear was playing a joke. Not a very nice joke, at that. The Blankets gave each person the strength to say, "Go away Fear! I don't want you around anymore!"

When the Blankets of White Light weren't needed any longer, they could be folded and stored in a pocket for the next time Trickster Fear came around.

One afternoon after the children had gone home, a new visitor walked up the path to Grandmother Hattie's cottage. The stranger was a beautiful angel. She had short, pink, curly hair and a face the color of pearls. Her flowing dress was made of Queen Anne's lace, and a wide berry colored sash wrapped around her tiny waist. Her large wings shimmered like iridescent fish scales. Fool had never seen an angel and he was a bit surprised, but Grandmother Hattie nodded a greeting. "Come sit with us," she invited, "tell us your name."

"Thank you," said the angel politely. "I will sit for just a moment, although I have many stops to make today. I've come to hold your hand while you begin your journey into the next adventure. My name is Death."

"No!" yelled Fool. "You can't take Grandmother Hattie! Everyone needs her! The children! Me! Everyone!"

"Hush," said Grandmother Hattie reaching over to stroke Fool's sandy hair. "Listen to what the angel has to say."

Soft and not at all scary, the angel didn't look anything like the hooded death characters grownups seemed so worried about. And she smelled like strawberry punch. Fool began to relax... just a little.

"Well," the Angel of Death began gently, "it's just that Grandmother Hattie has done a fine job here in the Village of Dreams. Now it is her time to travel to a land of great beauty and joy. She will have wonderful adventures, and she will learn some new, and very special stories. The trip will be fun for her. It is truly a gift to be invited to travel with me."

Fool was not totally convinced. He paced the wooden porch biting his stubby fingernails. "But what about Trickster Fear? If Grandmother Hattie is not around to weave her Blankets, and if she's not here to wrap them around people, Trickster Fear will be able to scare people so much that they will all become frozen! They won't be able to move or protect themselves from harm! And... and.... besides that, who will tell the stories?" Fool stomped his foot very hard on the porch. "You must not take Grandmother Hattie!"

"He has a point," said Grandmother Hattie. "What about the Blankets of White Light? Who will weave them, and who will wrap them around frightened people? And who *will* tell the stories?"

"Hmmmm," said the angel. "I do see the problem. Well, I guess we'll have to do something about that. Let's go for a walk," she said. "Walking is good for thinking."

So Grandmother Hattie and the Angel of Death strolled hand in hand down the path, leaving Fool to pick up the cookie plates and to pace worriedly back and forth on the big wooden porch.

A few hours later, arms linked and laughing like two old friends, the Angel of Death and Grandmother Hattie returned to the magical cottage. The angel said good-bye just before dinner time. Turning to leave, she winked at Grandmother Hattie and smiled gently at Fool.

"In love, my dears," she whispered, and was gone.

"Phew! I'm really glad that's over! She had me worried!" Fool breathed a sigh of relief. Grandmother Hattie didn't say anything. Humming an old song she had learned as a little girl, she began to wash all the dishes and fold all the linen in her magical cottage.

The next day, when the children once again settled with cookies and drinks, Grandmother Hattie leaned forward and said, "Children, tonight I will go on a long journey. It is my time, and I am very happy to be going. I want to tell you this so that you can help me to carry out my work." The children listened carefully. They knew this was an important assignment.

"From now on, since I will not be here, it will be your job, the job of all the children of the world, to wrap Blankets of White Light around anyone who is frightened or tricked by Trickster Fear. Sometimes this will be a hard job because Fear tricks people into believing that nothing can help them. But you children know how the Blankets of White Light work. Wrap them lovingly around anyone who needs one, and be sure to wear yours whenever you need it."

"But," asked one small girl sitting at the edge of the yard, "where will we get these blankets? You will not be around to weave them from your long hair."

Grandmother Hattie's eyes sparkled. "Tonight when you go to sleep, you will all have a very special dream, and then you will have the answer to your question! Now," she said, "come by and stroke my hair one last time, and give old Grandmother Hattie a big hug before you run along home."

Fool stood back at the edge of the porch looking very sad, indeed. After all the children had gone, Grandmother Hattie turned to him with great love in her eyes. "Don't be so sad, my dear young friend. You have a very important job to do, and you must be happy when you do it."

"What job?" sniffled Fool, trying hard to hold back his tears.

"*You*, Fool, will be the storyteller. You will be an adventurer. Go into the unknown, leap into the universe seeking new stories, and telling old ones to any and all who need to hear. The stories are important; they must be passed along. I'm depending on you, and I will always be close to you to help you if you need me.

I will be one of your guides, and you will be able to call on me anytime you need help, or anytime you begin to forget just how very much you are loved. Now, be a good friend and help me sweep out the cottage. We have many adventures ahead of us." Saying this, she turned and went inside. She was humming the old song again, and her long silver hair trailed behind like the veil of a young, happy bride.

Part II : The Night Ride

The children felt excited as they fell asleep that night because they knew something very special was happening in the Village of Dreams. As the moon rose in the velvet sky they found themselves standing at the edge of a lake in the middle of the forest. One by one they arrived, rubbing their eyes and yawning big yawns. At last they were gathered together by the water's edge. They stood holding hands, hugging each other, or just yawning. Shortly after Fool arrived and joined the children, a rustling began in the forest leaves. Out of the woods stepped a beautiful, silken and gentle white wolf. Although amazed, the children were not afraid. Riding sidesaddle on the back of the wolf, looking quite charming indeed, was Grandmother Hattie! Her pale blue dress shimmered, and her toes wiggled inside soft blue slippers. A blue lace ribbon, tied in a perfect bow, circled her neck. Her hair, longer now than ever, flowed over her shoulders, off the wolf, and onto the forest floor. Wearing a halter of calla lilies and violets, the wolf stepped close to the ring of children. Grandmother Hattie began to speak, her eyes twinkling like Christmas tree lights.

"Hello, my dears," she said. "I'm pleased that you could all come tonight. Like every child alive, you are all good, gentle beings. Once in a while, you feel confused and frightened. Sometimes you feel real fear. Real fear is a warning, a guide to let you know that something needs changing. At other times you feel the fear of the Trickster. The Trickster tries to use fear to confuse you, to freeze you, so that you won't know what to do. Real fear is helpful, but the fear of the Trickster is not much use at all."

"How will we know the difference?" one of the children asked.

Grandmother Hattie paused and looked lovingly into the eyes of each of the children. "When you are confused," she continued softly, "wrap a Blanket of White Light around yourself, get very still and go inside your heart. When you are warm and safe inside your own heart, ask yourself if this fear is real, or if it is a joke of the Trickster. Listen quietly for the answer. You will learn to know the difference. Your heart will tell you what to do. Trust your heart; it will never trick you. From this night forward, you children, and all the children of the world, will be in charge of the Blankets of White Light. Whenever you meet someone who is feeling fear, wrap a Blanket of White Light around them. They, and you, will be warm and safe from the fear of the Trickster."

"But, Grandmother Hattie," the boy with the dark brown skin spoke, "if you are not around to weave the Blankets, how will we get them?"

She laughed, "You will see. Now, my dear ones, know that you are loved very much, that you are loved every moment of every day, and that you are loved every moment of every night. You are never without my love. You are safe, and you are very, very good."

"One last thing," she said, turning toward Fool. "This is for you." She held out a staff carved from the wood of a Mountain Ash tree. Tied to the end of the staff was a brown leather bag. "You will need this as you travel through the universe on your journeys. It holds the memory of all things past, and the hope of all things yet to come." Fool stepped up to the wolf and took the gift from his dear old friend.

"Blessed Fool," said Grandmother Hattie, "now you are, indeed, the adventurer. *You* are the storyteller. Go. Travel. Be free. Have fun and know that my love is always with you."

With that she gave a little tug on the wolf's floral leash. Instantly the wolf took a giant leap and soared into the air. Holding firmly onto the string of lilies, Grandmother Hattie flew high across the night sky. Laughing happily, she rode the wolf in large rings over the forest lake. Her silver hair streamed out longer and longer behind her. As the wolf circled the lake above the forest, Grandmother Hattie's hair brushed the tops of the trees. Knowing exactly what to do, the trees joined together and became a giant loom weaving the silvery threads of hair into long, shining strips of moonlight. The wolf and Grandmother Hattie circled

the forest over and over and over again while the trees continued to weave her shining hair.

The moon was huge and full, and the children stood on the banks of the lake laughing, clapping and staring into the sky as they watched the magnificent ride. Finally the old woman and the wolf spiraled up high, high, very high over the trees and sailed way above the forest. Grandmother Hattie turned and waved once to the children, then she, and the wolf, flew so high they became just a tiny dot against the moon. At last the dot disappeared. At that very moment a shimmering moonbeam of white and silver light came drifting through the night sky. Carefully woven into the moonbeam were thousands of beautiful Blankets of White Light. As the moonbeam flowed from above, the Blankets fell in soft folds right into the hearts of the children standing below. The children knew then how they would always have the love and caring of Grandmother Hattie. Whenever someone needed protection from the cold of Trickster Fear, the children had only to reach into their own hearts and to pull out a magical Blanket of White Light.

One by one, as the children felt the moonbeam drift into their hearts, they found themselves tucked safely in their own beds at home. Bright morning sunlight streamed into their windows and gently kissed them awake.

Fool's Journey

<u>Where Fool meets Intuit, takes a boat ride, and
goes swimming with magical, talking fish.</u>

"Come on Fool, you can't just sit here on the porch day after day acting so glum." Kitonga, the dark boy from the forest, gently pressed against his friend. "You've got to get up. Grandmother Hattie wanted you to be the storyteller. She wanted you to go and do things! It's time for you to move, to change!" He nudged his friend again.

Sitting on the porch steps, elbows on his knees, and head in his hands, Fool breathed a long, sad sigh. "It's just that I miss Grandmother Hattie so much. I miss combing her long white hair; I miss the stories. You just don't know how I feel; you just don't know." He sighed again.

"Yes, I do know!" Nodding his head up and down, Kitonga went on. "We all miss Grandmother Hattie. We all miss her stories, her long hair. We even miss the way she smelled. But she's enjoying someplace else now. She's having new adventures. It's time for us to start some new adventures of our own. You know," he said, looking sideways at his friend, "that's what she told us to do. That's what she wanted us to do."

"You're right, of course," Fool answered glumly, "but I just don't seem to have the energy to do anything."

Early morning sunlight played with the tight black curls on Kitonga's head. The two boys sat quietly for a while, each thinking about the days they'd spent listening to Grandmother Hattie tell her magical stories. Absently, Fool twirled the long red feather in his cap. Kitonga stared at his toes poking from his leather sandals.

Standing up to leave, Kitonga encouraged Fool. "What you need is a little push, something to get you going." Leaning over he gave his friend a gentle squeeze on the shoulder. The two friends smiled at each other. Kitonga stepped off the porch and walked down the path leading from Grandmother Hattie's magical cottage. Reaching the end, he turned and waved to his friend.

"Good luck, Fool. Have adventures and let Intuition be your guide!" Whistling happily, he rounded a corner and vanished.

"He's right," mumbled Fool. "I really do need to get up and get going again. Maybe a walk down by the river will help." Packing a small sandwich from Grandmother Hattie's kitchen into his jacket pocket, Fool put on his cap, picked up his staff and carefully locked the cottage door. Moving slowly, head hung low in sadness, Fool shuffled along toward the river that flowed through the forest by Grandmother Hattie's magical cottage. Half-way there, he heard loud barking.

"Ark, ark, ark!" It was a little yellow dog with a fluffy yellow tail curling up over his back like an ostrich feather. His white paws were fuzzy bedroom slippers, and white chest fur looked like a dinner napkin tied around his neck. Happy, dark brown eyes sparkled, and his cold black nose twitched constantly.

"Good dog! What a good boy!" said Fool bending down to pet the shaggy creature. Wiggling his entire body, the dog stretched up and planted a great big, sloppy, wet dog kiss right on Fool's cheek.

"Yuck!" laughed Fool, wiping the kiss from his face. "Are you someone's pet?" Reaching down to stroke the dog again, Fool searched through the thick hair for a collar and tags. Underneath the fluffy fur the dog was very skinny. Hanging from a loose collar, a single red tag in the shape of a heart spelled, 'INTUIT'. "You don't seem to have a home little buddy." At Fool's words the wriggling stopped, and the dog's tail drooped toward the ground. "Ahhh, don't worry fellow," comforted Fool. "Here, take this," he said, holding out his sandwich. Intuit grabbed the food and gulped it down without pausing to sniff it.

"Come with me," said Fool, turning toward the Village of Dreams. "Maybe we can find a home for you." But Intuit had very different ideas. Leaving Fool, he scampered down the forest path toward the river. "Wait, little dog! Wait!" yelled Fool as he began running after the quickly disappearing yellow tail.

Gasping for breath, Fool finally caught up with the little dog. Intuit stood next to a small green rowboat bobbing lightly in the calm water at the river's edge. His tail wagged round in circles, and he grinned a doggy smile that stretched from ear to floppy ear.

A tan colored rope, that should have tied the boat to a pier or tree, dangled lazily in the water. "I've never seen this boat," Fool told the dog. "I come down to the river all the time, but this boat has never been here before. We'd better go into the village to find its owner. But first, we should row the boat over to a tree and tie it so it won't drift away." As if in agreement, Intuit danced around in circles, chasing his tail and barking loudly.

Rolling up his pants and holding his shoes and staff high in the air, Fool ventured into the water. Wading out to the boat and climbing carefully into the small craft, he managed to keep fairly dry. The inside of the boat was neat and tidy. A new coat of white paint smelled fresh and clean. Pale green seat cushions rested on two narrow wooden seats. Finding the oars missing, he decided to climb out and use the rope to pull the boat to a nearby tree. As Fool began to climb out, Intuit dashed through the water and tried to jump into the boat.

"Ark, Ark," he barked, jumping and splashing at the side of the bobbing vessel.

"Stop it!" shouted Fool. "You're getting me all wet! Now you just stop it! I need to get out so I can tie this to a tree!"

But Intuit continued to jump up and down against the boat. As he did, he began to push the small craft away from the still waters beside the shore and toward the rushing waters in the center of the river.

"Stop it! You're pushing me into the current!" yelled Fool, but it was too late. The river tugged and pulled at the little boat. "Oh, no! Now look what you've done! I'm heading into the middle!" Just then Intuit made one more giant leap and landed half in and half out of the boat. Grabbing Intuit's collar and pulling with all his might, Fool yanked the soaking wet dog into the boat. Tumbling to the floor boards, he and Intuit made a tangled, messy, and very wet, bundle.

"Get off me, you dummy dog!" sputtered Fool trying to free himself from the wet animal. Standing up and shaking his fur from nose to tail, Intuit sent a fine spray of water all over Fool. Unnoticed as the boy and the dog were shaking and dripping water over each other, the little boat gained speed and sailed downstream at a very fast pace.

"Hold on!" yelled Fool, grabbing the sides of the boat. Intuit jumped to the front, planted his wet hind feet on a green cushion and hung his front paws over the bow. Yellow fur flying, he barked into the wind. He was the happiest dog in the world!

Whirling round and round, the tiny boat sped down the river. Trees, stumps and boulders raced by as Intuit barked joyfully at the top of his doggy lungs. Startled by the noise, a box turtle snapped his head into his shell with a quick plop. A tall white bird with skinny legs rose quickly from her nest making a giant whooshing sound. Despite being hurled through the water at great speed, Fool began having fun. Holding onto the boat with one hand and waving his hat high with the other, Fool rode the bouncing boat like a cowboy riding a bucking bronco. "Yipppeeeeee!" he hollered into the wind as the boat raced over bounding, rushing waves. "Yippeeee!"

Eventually, the river calmed and the waters smoothed. Slowing down, the boat drifted lazily along the old stream. Looking around, Fool noticed that his river, the river that flowed through the forest by Grandmother Hattie's cottage, was about to join with another small river. Together, the two rivers created a deep, wide, band of dark, green water.

A narrow peninsula of land jutted out between the two small rivers. Covered with pine trees and berry bushes, the peninsula looked safe and inviting. Drifting gently toward the land, the boat moved into shallow waters until it scraped lightly against the sandy bottom and stopped.

"Ya hoo! We've landed!" called Fool, jumping out of the boat. Grabbing the boat's rope, he pulled it a short way onto the sandy beach. Intuit immediately scrambled out, splashed through the shallow water, and began running all over, from here to there, happily sniffing each bush and tree.

Leaning his staff against a tree, Fool walked around exploring and picking hundreds of fat, dark purple berries. Each berry, shaped like a sewing thimble, was juicy and sweet. Hungry after the boat ride, Fool and Intuit ate the delicious berries until their smiles were curling purple ribbons painted on happy faces. Tired and full of berries, the two friends lay down on a patch of warm, golden sand under a pine tree and slipped into peaceful afternoon naps. While the two friends slept, the sun moved gracefully across the sky painting shadows on the land as it traveled.

Loud barking woke Fool just in time for him to see the little green boat go drifting out of sight. While he and Intuit were sleeping, the waves, gently lapping at the stern of the boat, had eased it off the sandy beach into the river's current.

"Well that's just great. Now what?" Fool asked himself. Dismayed and thirsty, he walked to the shore for a cool, clear drink. Lying on his belly gulping the icy water, Fool heard Intuit barking again.

"Ark, Ark, Ark!"

"What is it, boy?" asked Fool, looking up. There before him, leaping, twisting and glistening in the sunlight were three huge, magnificent fish. Jumping out of the river high into the air and crashing back into the rushing water, they splashed Fool and Intuit. With shining scales of pink, coral and silver, they were clearly the most beautiful fish that Fool had ever seen.

"Oh! You are soooooo beautiful," called Fool.

"Thank you," said one of the fish, diving a double twist into the river.

"Oh, fish, what name do you call yourselves?"

"We are salmon," laughed a second fish, slapping the surface of the river, getting Intuit quite wet.

"Salmon, what is the name of this river?" asked Fool.

"We swim up the River of Time to our homeland. Come little Fool, and come little Fool's dog, swim up the river with us. As we travel we will tell you the story of our homeland and how it began."

Intrigued by the beautiful fish, Fool and Intuit jumped into the river and began swimming with the Salmon. This is the story the pink, coral and silver fish told Fool and Intuit as they swam upstream in the River of Time.

Chapter Two

Katie Cass and The Land Just Slightly North of Heaven

Many, many moons ago, a young goddess named Katie Cass lived with her Aunt Mojave in a part of the universe located Just Slightly North of Heaven. Katie's dark brown skin softly framed her slate blue eyes. Shimmering silver hair fell in ripples around her shoulders. Her clothing was as pretty as her sweet face. Like the first daffodils of spring, a bright yellow dress poked out from under her dark green velvet cape.

In The Land Just Slightly North of Heaven, all the young gods and goddesses shared the job of caretaking the land. Their chores played an important role in growing up. Some were in charge of planting fields of wheat or corn. Others stirred the oceans to create tides and currents. A few watered the plants by shaking rain clouds over the earth. Katie Cass held the responsibility of tidying up and taking care of the flat, marshy bog land which served as home to her many pets. Squirrels, deer, elk, owls, bears, butterflies, opossum and hundreds of other creatures lived together comfortably under Katie's loving care. Of course, today these kinds of animals don't live in bogs, they live in forests... but that's getting ahead of the story.

Katie felt confident about her ability to take care of the animals and their swampy home. Every morning she watered the bog to keep it wet and marshy. Each afternoon she walked ever so gently over the moist earth to make it low and flat. Goddesses, even when they are young, are very, very large and just one footprint covers many miles of land. As Katie walked carefully over the swampy land, she smiled at all the happy animals living in the peaceful bog.

One sunny afternoon a large violet envelope arrived in the mail. Inside, a card decorated with balloons and streamers invited Katie to a birthday party.

Clapping her hands in excitement, Katie hurried off to ask Aunt Mojave for permission to attend. "Parties are so much fun and birthday cake is my favorite!" She asked her aunt, "May I go, please, please?"

"Of course," replied Aunt Mojave, "but first you must take care of your little pets and their homes in the bog. After you clean the grounds, bring in fresh water and carefully smooth the land, we can leave for the party."

"But, Auntie," whined Katie, "that will take hours and the party will be almost over before I even arrive!"

"Nonsense," said her aunt, a kind but very practical goddess, "your duties come first. Take care of the land and your little pets. You know Katie," she reminded her young niece, "when you do your chores with love, even the hardest jobs are fun and go by quickly! That is the Way of the Goddess. There will be plenty of time for parties when your chores are done."

"I won't!" screamed Katie. "I want to go to the party now!" Flying back to the bog in a rage, she threw the very biggest temper tantrum any child had thrown for a long, long time. "I want to play first!" she yelled, and stomped her feet in the bog. Now remember... to grown up gods and goddesses Katie's feet seemed small, but to the earth below, they appeared huge. "I just _won't_ do my chores!" she shouted, kicking the ground. Smashing her feet down hard, she sent huge sprays of brown mud flying out in all directions. Giant holes formed in her foot-prints and mounds of slippery sludge piled into mountains of dripping, slimy goo. Flying mud and moss and splashing goush turned the once dreamy bog into a nightmare. "I won't, I won't, I won't! I want my own way now!" She screamed, jumping up and down in her fury. The world below her goddess feet churned and splashed and twisted.

Running for dear life, big and little animals scattered as their homes fell trampled and destroyed under her rage.

Katie clenched her fat little goddess fists so tightly that lightning bolts flew out of them and lit swamp gas on fire. The bog belched flames and spit huge squirts of mud. It was the most frightening and horrible temper tantrum ever seen in The Land Just Slightly North of Heaven.

Just as Katie was about to stomp her heel into another part of the marsh, she heard a loud squeal. "Stoooop Katie, please stop! You'll kill my babies!" Her foot in mid-air, Katie stopped and looked down to the earth below. Mother Squirrel stood on the edge of her nest flinging her arms wide to shield six terrified and very, very tiny baby squirrels huddled behind her. "Please, Katie Cass, don't crush my babies!" Mother Squirrel begged. "You've ruined the entire bog. All our homes are gone forever, but let my babies live!"

"Oh, no!" gasped Katie, gently lowering her foot away from the nest. "What have I done?" She looked around her beloved bog. A massive battle zone of deep holes and mounds of sloppy mud replaced the once calm and peaceful swamp. Frightened, wounded animals scrambled around in terror and confusion trying to avoid raging fires. "Oh, no! What have I done?" she repeated.

Katie sat down beside the bog and began to cry. "I've destroyed my little pets and their happy homes. My anger and selfishness have destroyed the very things I love so much. Oh, I'm so very sorry," she sobbed. Taking off her cape she spread it gently over the land, smothering the destructive fires. Her quiet weeping sent tears flowing over the crevasses and folds of her dark green cape to soak through the soft, deep velvet.

About this time Aunt Mojave stopped by to check on Katie's progress with her chores and to take her to the party. Immediately, Aunt Mojave realized what had happened. She could see what Katie had done, and she could feel Katie's sadness. Aunt Mojave knew that Katie truly loved her little pets and the land that was their home. She also knew that in all the universe, the one thing that heals pain and sadness is true love. So, with the grace and wisdom of a gentle goddess, she waved her large and powerful arm over Katie, the cape, and the destroyed landscape. Slowly, tears soaking through the cape became tiny streams and then strong, wide rivers. The dark green velvet melted into the muddy land and started to grow.

Lush, deep forests with clear flowing rivers replaced the destruction of Katie's temper tantrum. Where mud once slid in gooey mounds, towering mountains formed. Meadows of flowers, the color of Katie's dress, sprang up replacing the marshy swamp. Tall green trees stretched toward the sky and purple vines crept over the ground. Clouds floating by brushed against Katie's hair taking on its silvery cast. A slate blue sky reflected her tear filled eyes. The land changed from flat, swampy bog to rich mountain forest.

One by one the little animals came out of hiding. "I can live in this new land," said one.

"Me too," chirped another.

"Yes, we can live in the trees," squeaked the baby squirrels.

"And we can have fun swimming in the rivers!" said the bog fish.

"Come now, dear," said Aunt Mojave offering Katie a tissue. "Dry your eyes and help your little friends adjust to their new homes. They will feel your love, and love helps to heal all sadness."

From that day forward Katie Cass grew into a lovely and extremely wise young goddess. She went to lots of parties. In fact, she became a very popular goddess. But before she played, she always took care of the land. And she told her story to her friends so they would remember that work done joyfully and lovingly goes by quickly, while anger and selfishness can destroy the very things we love most.

As a reminder of her lesson, the forests and mountains were named after Katie Cass. Today The Land Just Slightly North of Heaven is called the Cascade Mountain Range. Aunt Mojave considered the name a fitting tribute, for she remembered a similar incident that had taken place in her own childhood. But *that*'s another story.

Fool's Journey

Where Fool and Intuit try to swim upstream, get trapped
in the Ballard fish ladder, and are rescued by the
lockmaster and his gentle wife, Katrina.

"Great story, Salmon!" Fool called out to the fish as he, Intuit, and the salmon swam upstream in the River of Time. "But, you know," he panted, "I'm getting tired from all this swimming, and it's almost evening. When will we get to your homeland?"

"Around the bend and we're there!" laughed the biggest fish, who never tired of swimming against the strong current. Just to show off, the silvery fish jumped high and twirled around three times then splashed into the icy waters. Before Fool could speak another word, the river curved and placed the swimmers directly in front of a giant staircase. Cascading water spilled down each large step.

"Ark, ark!" barked Intuit, clearly worried about the idea of swimming up a staircase in cold, rushing water. The river roared and thundered, sending thousands of tons of water over and down the huge steps.

"What's that?" yelled Fool, trying to be heard over the noise.

"Oh, that's the fish ladder," answered one of the salmon. "This river flows down a large hill. We jump up fish ladders to get from the low part of the river to calmer waters at the summit. That's where we gather to spawn." Flinging himself into the air, the fish easily landed on the first giant step.

"See you at the top!" he called, leaping and gliding toward the second enormous step. Glancing around, Fool saw that Intuit's brown eyes were as big and round as bicycle tires.

"Hang in there, Intuit!" he called to his frightened friend. "We can do it. Just follow the salmon!" With that, Fool tried leaping up the fish ladder after the silver and coral fish.

SPLAT! He fell smack back into the river, landing flat on his belly. Yelling "OUCH!" only made matters worse, as rushing water filled his mouth. "Glub, plub, plub!" Sputtering and spitting out water, Fool paddled around in a frenzy looking for Intuit. Spinning in a circle, he spotted Intuit bent half way over the first stair. Trying to jump up the slippery steps, Intuit had made it only part way there. The poor little dog held on bravely with his two front legs while his skinny back legs paddled out into the air with all their might. Giving a mighty roar, the river finally pushed him off the stair, plummeting him into the swirling water below. For a moment, the dog disappeared beneath the surface.

Fool panicked. "Intuit! Intuit! Where are you, boy?" he yelled frantically, turning every which way in the water looking for his friend. Suddenly Intuit's drenched head popped up. Coughing and spitting out water, he splashed around searching for Fool.

Panicked, cold, and nearly exhausted, the two friends were becoming very, very frightened. In growing despair Fool called out to the fish for help, but they were busy climbing the ladder. It seemed they had forgotten their little companions.

Trying to call encouragement to Intuit, Fool's mouth again filled with water. Choking and sputtering, he felt the river push him under once, then twice.

"Help! Help!" he called, as he came to the surface splashing at the swirling water. Eyes barely above the surface, he spotted Intuit paddling as fast as his tired legs could go, trying to stay above the rapidly surging water. Mouth, ears and nose filled, and for a third time he was sucked beneath the engulfing wetness.

For a moment Fool's world became completely empty. He stopped thinking and, briefly, he even stopped feeling. The very next moment he felt himself being lifted out of the water with Intuit squashed against him, his staff poking into his back. Squirming around, Fool realized that he and Intuit were in some kind of giant net and that they were being lifted high into the air.

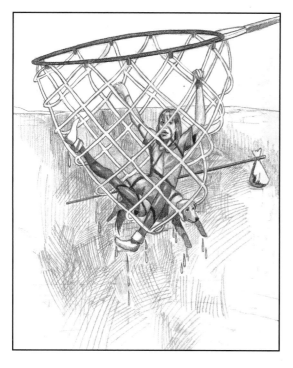

"Ho! Ho! What's this I've fished from the water today? A very wet doggy, and an even wetter boy! Or else they are very strange fish!"

Kerplunk! Fool and Intuit tumbled onto a wooden dock. Spilling from the net, the two companions squirted water from their noses and mouths.

"Sven! Sven! What is it you've got there?" Fool heard a woman's voice calling to the large man holding the net. Not waiting for her husband to answer, the woman hurried out of a small house. Fool watched her bustling toward them.

"Why, good heavens, Sven, it's a child!" she exclaimed, reaching the dock. "And a dog! And they're wet and half frozen! Hurry! Bring them to the house so we can get them dry and warm."

Joining her husband, the woman reached down and together they grabbed Fool under the arms and pulled him up off the ground.

"C'mon, little guy, Katrina's gonna take care of you and that's the best care in the world! You can tell us what happened once you're dried out."

Stumbling and shivering, Fool followed the couple into their red brick home built at the top of the fish ladder, right next to the river. Intuit followed, pausing every few steps to shake fine sprays of water over the couple and his already drenched friend.

Tiny and cozy, the cheerful house offered safety and warmth. A crackling fire filling a large fireplace sent its light to every corner. Hurrying to the fire, Fool and Intuit stood dripping and shivering.

"Sven, mind your manners and bring out some of Jon's old clothes. Let's get the child dried and dressed. I'm going to pour some big bowls of stew for these frozen swimmers." Katrina, a short, round woman with blond braids twisted up and around her head, wore a long white apron covered with flour from baking and food stains from cooking over her woollen dress. Even though she seemed to be fussing all the time, she was gentle and loving. Fool liked her right away.

"Here you go." Smiling, Katrina's husband handed Fool a pile of dry clothes. "You can change in the back room. These won't fit you, of course, they belong to our son, Jon. He's twice your size. A strapping fellow!" Beaming with pride, he added, "Jon's off to see the world — joined the Navy!"

As Fool changed clothes, the cheerful man happily dried Intuit with heavy, terry cloth towels.

Soon warming himself on a three legged stool in front of the fire, his borrowed clothes rolled up at the sleeves and cuffs and a length of boat rope tied around his waist to hold up the trousers, Fool breathed a sigh of relief. His own clothes hung, dripping, on wooden pegs next to the fireplace. Scooping up large spoonfuls of delicious, steaming hot stew and munching on warm, homemade potato bread, Fool began to feel safe and secure. Sitting beside Fool, Intuit made sloppy, slurping noises as he chewed a soup bone. While Fool and Intuit ate, the kindly rescuers introduced themselves.

"Sven Svenson, and this is my wife Katrina," the man offered. "I'm the lockmaster. Katrina and I, we tend to the locks and keep the fish ladder in good repair."

"I know about fish ladders now," said Fool. "But what are locks?" he asked between mouthfuls. Pleased to talk about his work, Mr. Svenson eagerly explained that locks allow boats to move up steep sections of the river, letting the water do all the work. Unlike salmon, boats (and swimming dogs and boys!) require more than arching backs

and flashing, powerful tails to overcome the river's swift steep slopes up hills and mountains.

"The way it works," he went on, "boats enter a small, boxed off area of the river. Two of the walls are made of concrete. Two large steel doors, one at each end of the box, open and close electronically. That's my job, to control the opening and closing of the lock doors." Obviously pleased with his job, Sven glowed as he continued. "Once boats are safely inside the box, with both doors closed, water is allowed to flow from the higher parts of the river into the box. As the box fills with water, the boats float until they are at the same level as the water up river. When the boats reach the correct level, the front door is opened and the boats sail out! It's all very simple, once you understand the principle." Sven puffed up with pride as he shared his knowledge of rivers and locks.

"Enough about work, Sven!" Turning to Fool, Katrina smiled gently and asked, "Now, child. Who are you, and what happened to you?" Setting the stew bowl down, and neatly wiping his mouth on a napkin, Fool told the lockmaster and Katrina all about his adventures. He told them about Grandmother Hattie, and how he had become the storyteller. He told them about meeting Intuit and their crazy ride down the river. And he told them about meeting the magical fish and swimming upstream in the River of Time.

As Fool related his adventures, Katrina held a hankie to her mouth from time to time as if to hold in a giggle. Looking over at her husband several times, she caught him winking at her.

Finishing his tale, Fool looked across at his hosts and announced, "So, here I am, wherever this is."

"Well, child," answered the kindly woman, "you're in Ballard. It's a small city built next to this stretch of the river. You'll see more of it tomorrow. Ballard is a friendly place with friendly people. You might really like it here! For now, you must be very, very tired, just like your puppy there." Curled up on the rug in front of the fire, Intuit's eyes were barely open. His moist fur steamed in the warmth of the fire.

"I am tired, Mr. and Mrs. Svenson," answered Fool earnestly. "But you both have been so kind, I feel I need to do something to repay your kindness. Perhaps I could tell you one of the stories I learned from Grandmother Hattie. It will be sure to bring you wonderful, sweet dreams tonight. Would you like that?" Looking at each other, the couple nodded.

"Of course, sweetheart," answered Mrs. Svenson. "We'd love to hear one of your grandma's stories."

The toasty fire crackled and popped. Falling asleep, Intuit began to snore softly. Mr. Svenson filled his pipe with sweet smelling tobacco, and Mrs. Svenson knitted thick woolen stockings for her husband. As the magical salmon splashed and spawned in the river next to the snug little home of Sven and Katrina, Fool told the gentle people the story of 'Beth and Her Friend From Space.'

Chapter Three

<u>The Story of Beth and Her Friend From Space</u>

"Hey, Beth! Karen has a new video game. Wanna go play it?" Beth looked up from her book.

"No, Roslyn," she told her sister, "you go. I want to finish reading."

"You spend too much time reading," Roslyn teased her. "You're gonna turn into a bookworm!" Laughing, she skipped out of the room.

Beth sat on the floor and leaned against her bed. Sunlight streaming in the window made patterns on the pale blue carpeting. Closing her eyes to rest them for a moment, she fell fast asleep.

Suddenly, Beth's eyes flew open. She was completely surprised! The most unusual creature she had ever seen sat directly in front of her. Beth rubbed her eyes, but it did not go away. It was white... sort of pearly white. Thin and smooth with no hair, no clothes, no wrinkles or lines of any kind, it sat quietly. Big, dark eyes, the shape of huge almonds focused on her. "Wow!" whispered Beth. Totally amazed, she forgot to be afraid. Beth and the creature just sat and stared at each other.

"Honey, do you know where your sister is?"

Beth turned her head toward the door to answer her mother.

"At Karen's house playing video games," she answered, blinking her eyes. When she turned back, the creature was gone.

Everyday after school Beth went upstairs and sat on the floor next to her bed, hoping the creature would return. She didn't tell her family about it because Roslyn would have teased her, and her parents would have said, "It's perfectly normal for children to have imaginary friends. You'll grow out of this phase soon!" Beth could never understand why grownups would not believe the things children told

them. Just because *they* couldn't see faeries, angels and other creatures, parents assumed these things weren't real. Beth knew there was more to the world than video games and television. And she was sure there was a whole lot more than what grownups usually saw. But, after a week of waiting, she began to doubt herself and she began to be glad she hadn't told anyone else.

One night, very late, when the moon was full and round, Beth woke to a still and quiet house. Roslyn's light snoring and the ticking of the downstairs hall clock were the only sounds she could hear. Getting up, wrapping herself in her quilt, Beth sat on the floor next to the bed. In an instant the creature sat cross-legged in front of her. Thrilled, Beth wanted to talk, but she didn't want to wake Roslyn.

"Just think the thoughts," something in her mind seemed to say. She looked into the eyes of the gentle creature.

"Did that come from you?" She thought the words but didn't say anything out loud.

"Yes! Yes!" she heard in her mind. Happy and excited, Beth somehow knew the creature was feeling the same way.

"What's your name, and where are you from?" she thought.

The words 'Frederick' and 'space' floated into her mind.

"Oh," she smiled to herself. "His name is Frederick. I'm talking with a space creature named Frederick! This seems so silly!"

"And just imagine," she heard the creature think, "I'm talking with a little girl from Earth!" Sitting in the moonlight Beth and Frederick shared a wonderful feeling of giggles and laughter.

Looking at Frederick, Beth thought, "You are beautiful. You remind me of a pearly plastic button!" The very second she thought those words, her mind filled with a picture of herself in a large swimming pool overflowing with white plastic buttons. She laughed and swam and splashed in them. Tossing handfuls into the air and floating on her back, Beth became a dolphin in a sparkling sea of white foam. Safe, happy, and silly, she played in the pool of buttons.

The next thing she knew her mother was shaking her. "And what are you doing sleeping on the floor young lady?" she asked, rushing out the door without waiting for an answer.

Beth yawned; time to get ready for school. Pushing to her feet, she glanced down at the floor. There, shining in the morning sun, was one pearly white plastic button.

After school that day, Beth decided to pay a visit to Ida, the old woman who lived across the street. All the kids on the street liked her. She used a walker to get around, smelled like cherry flavored medicine, and kept a big dish of fresh fruit by her door. Ida was the only grownup who believed the children when they told her about faeries, dragons, angels and monsters.

Munching on a shiny red apple, Beth told Ida all about Frederick. She discussed the happy feeling she had whenever Frederick came by, and how they seemed to talk by just thinking words. Ida listened very carefully. "And he gave me this," Beth said, dropping the button into Ida's wrinkled hand. Ida's fingers closed slowly around the button. "So, what do you think?" Beth asked.

The old woman shut her eyes and leaned back into her rocking chair. She didn't say anything for a long, long time. At last she opened her eyes and looked at Beth through her thick glasses.

"I think," she began, "that Frederick is a visitor from a place called 'The Pleiades' — it's way up in space. He's very happy that you can see him because not too many people from Earth can. He has a job to do, and he needs your help."

"A job?" Confused, Beth asked, "What kind of job, Ida?"

"I don't know, dear. I only know it has to do with Mr. Finestar." Then the old woman drifted off to sleep. The button slipped through her fingers and rolled to the floor. Picking it up, Beth tip-toed out of Ida's house.

"Why Mr. Finestar?" she wondered out loud as she skipped across the street to her own house for dinner.

Mr. Finestar, a scientist working in the government space program, lived down the street. He had turned his attic into an observatory, and every summer he invited people in the neighborhood to view stars from his telescope. The day after visiting Ida, Beth went to Mr. Finestar's house. Leaning her bike against his front porch, she heaved a big sigh.

"Well," she thought to herself, "here goes! I hope I'm doing the right thing!" At the very moment her finger touched the doorbell, Beth felt happy and contented. She knew that Frederick was near. Feeling reassured, she smiled.

"Hi there — Roslyn isn't it?" Mr. Finestar asked opening the door.

"No, that's my sister. I'm Beth."

"Well, yes, of course! You kids grow so fast I can't keep you straight! Selling cookies I bet — is it cookie time again already?"

"Umm, no, Mr. Finestar. I have to do a report for school and I want to write about The Pleiades. I wondered if you could give me some ideas."

"The Pleiades, is it?" Mr. Finestar rubbed his chin. "Well, I do have some star charts that show that constellation. Maybe you could take them to school. Come on, they're in the observatory."

Beth followed Mr. Finestar up the stairs to his attic. The observatory was wonderfully messy. Papers and books scattered everywhere. Charts spread out covering the floor. Pens, pencils and markers littered the desk. "Just give me a minute to find them," Mr. Finestar mumbled as he went searching through stacks of papers. "I saw them just the other day."

"Here's one," he said, holding up a huge folded chart. "I know there are a couple more — one in color I think — but let's take a look at this one first." As he started to unfold it, Beth noticed Frederick standing next to him.

"Ah, Mr. Finestar, did you know that there are... sort of... well, people who live in the Pleiades?"

Mr. Finestar pushed his glasses up on his nose and peered at the chart. "Of course, dear, some people think other life forms exist out there. I guess... I suppose it could be true, but in all my years in the space program, I've never seen one. Nope. Never saw one myself."

Beth looked from Mr. Finestar to where Frederick had been standing just a moment before. Frederick was gone. In his place stood a tall, stern looking creature resembling a grownup Frederick. He looked serious.

"Well, Mr. Finestar, you're going to see one today." Beth pointed to the tall creature. Mr. Finestar looked over his glasses at the young girl.

"Now don't let your imagination run away with you. You're probably just caught up in this school pro... Yeikes!" screeched Mr. Finestar as his eyes followed to where Beth pointed.

Jumping sideways and knocking over a chair, Mr. Finestar stumbled backwards. Running into a bookshelf he slid to the floor. Tumbling off shelves, books fell all over the frightened scientist. "Wha — wha — What is it? Stay away! I must be seeing things!"

Feeling safe and happy the way she did when Frederick was around, Beth also felt a bit sleepy. Slipping into her mind were the words, "Calm him down."

"Mr. Finestar, don't worry, I have a friend just like — well almost just like — this guy. They're really nice. I think he just wants to talk to you."

Despite being scared and confused, Mr. Finestar's curiosity began to take over. "What does he want to say?" he whispered to Beth, never taking his eyes off the tall creature.

"Just listen," she said. "Can't you hear him?"

"I've come with a message." The words floated softly into Beth's head.

"I can't hear anything except the pounding of my heart," Mr. Finestar answered. "You tell me what he's saying."

So Beth stood still and let the words drift into her head. As they came, she said them out loud for Mr. Finestar.

"I have come to let you know that we are quite concerned about what you are doing in your space experiments. We are very pleased that you want to know more about our home, but you are sending a great deal of pollution, noise, garbage and unpleasant energy into the space outside your planet. You probably don't know it, but space is our front yard. When you send things into space and don't retrieve them, it's very much like someone driving past your house and throwing bags of litter and cans and bottles out of their vehicle onto your yard. You would not like that, would you?" The words stopped. Beth felt so sleepy that she could hardly keep her eyes open.

She heard Mr. Finestar whisper, "No, I... I mean we... that is, of course, we didn't know and well..." Beth heard the words start again.

"So, we welcome you, and we will do anything we can to help you with your exploration. But, please, stop sending unhappy energy, pollution and noise into our home area. Please share this message with your co-workers in the space program. We would be most appreciative of this."

Mr. Finestar gulped. "Yes, of course," he said and nodded to the creature. Then the tall creature turned and looked directly at Beth. The words began, but this time they were soft and gentle.

"Our son, Frederick, did well to find you, young person from Earth. We are most pleased with him. We needed some help reaching this scientist, and we are grateful for your assistance. We must go home now, but we are sure Frederick will remember you through all time. In much peace, young one, we leave you now."

The room was still and quiet. Mr. Finestar and Beth just looked at each other. Finally, Mr. Finestar cleared his throat and stood up.

"Well, I... uh, guess I better go now," Beth said. "Mom gets upset if we're late for dinner."

"Right," Mr. Finestar replied, leading Beth to the front door. Neither of them really knew what to say. "Oh, I almost forgot, do you want the star charts?"

"Um, no," Beth answered. "Maybe I'll just do a different report or something. Thanks anyway."

"No problem," the scientist mumbled, closing the front door. Beth knew Mr. Finestar had some serious thinking to do!

Feeling very tired that night, Beth went to bed right after dinner. Snuggled under the covers she fell into a deep, relaxing sleep. Sometime in the middle of the night she woke up and stared at the moonlight that came pouring in through her bedroom window. Although she couldn't be quite certain, it did seem to her that on the floor, right by her bed, painted by a brush of moonlight, was the image of one, very lovely, pearly white button.

Fool's Journey

<u>Where Fool and Intuit hitch a ride with the
Amazing Donald and his hot air balloon show.</u>

"My goodness, child, that really was an, umm, imaginative story," Katrina said when Fool had finished. "But it's time we all got some sleep. Sven, would you bring out Jon's old sleeping bag for this child?" Mrs. Svenson patted Fool on the arm. "Pleasant dreams, young man," she said packing her knitting away.

"Good night, son. Glad you and the dog are alright." Mr. Svenson dropped the sleeping bag on the rug next to the fireplace.

"Thank you both," said Fool, unrolling the sleeping bag and slipping into its soft flannel lining. "You've been very kind."

As the couple left the room, Fool heard them whispering in low voices. "That boy certainly does have an imagination! Thinking he was the assistant to some magical old woman. And talking salmon!" The lockmaster shook his head. "Tomorrow we'll call the folks at the mayor's office. They can begin looking for his family."

Fool lay awake by the fire staring into the orange coals for a long time before sleeping. He was grateful to the Svensons for fishing him and Intuit out of the river, and he knew that they meant well. And, probably, the rest of the people in Ballard would be nice, too. But, Fool knew no matter how helpful they meant to be, the folks from the mayor's office would never really understand that he and Intuit were magical beings from the Land of Dreams. Rules and laws that make sense when people are awake don't always work with magical folk. With these thoughts dancing round and round in his head, Fool slipped into sleep, dreaming of a plan to continue his adventure.

Waking a few hours before dawn, Fool slipped out of the sleeping bag. Shivering in the early chill, he rolled the bag and stashed it neatly next to the fireplace. Cold ashes were all that remained of the evening's fire. The room was dark and still. Intuit snored peacefully. Quietly finding a small piece of paper and a pencil, Fool wrote a thank you note to the lockmaster and his wife. Leaving the note on a table, he quickly changed into his own, now dry clothing, picked up his staff, and softly patted Intuit on the head. Jumping up, Intuit almost started barking, but Fool put his arms around the dog and gave him a gentle hug. Intuit licked Fool's face and the two friends tiptoed quietly toward the door and let themselves out into the cold, gray morning air.

Moving rapidly away from the lockmaster's house, they traveled along city streets following the river. A fine misty rain drizzled over Fool, but he was so happy to be on another adventure that he barely noticed.

After an hour or so, Fool realized he was quite lost. Guessing that daylight was only a short time away he began to consider his options. "Exploring a city might be fun," Fool reasoned with Intuit. "But somehow, I just have a feeling that cities are not the best places for an adventurer and his dog. What do you think, boy?"

"Ark! Ark!" barked Intuit, prancing around Fool.

"Then it's agreed! We're on our way out of the city!"

Picking up their pace, they soon came to an enormous gas station with several large trucks lined up waiting to get fuel. One of the trucks looked especially interesting to Fool. That truck was carrying the biggest basket he had ever seen. A large sign on the side of the truck read:

> *Amazing Donald's Hot Air Balloon Show*
> *See the Lakes   See the Forests*
> *See the World from a Bird's Eye View!*
> *Special Rates for Children*

"See the forest," thought Fool, longing to be out of the city and back into the forest he loved so much.

"C'mon, boy," he said softly to Intuit, "let's take a balloon ride!" Going inside the station to pay for gas, the driver left his partner sitting in the truck's cab reading a newspaper. Sneaking carefully, Fool and Intuit scrambled into the back of the truck and climbed into the big basket. Filling the basket were all kinds of ropes and something that looked like a giant tent folded into hundreds of pleats. Fool quickly tucked his staff between two of the pleats.

"Hurry!" he whispered to Intuit. "Hide under some of this tent, and please, no barking!" Huddling low in the basket, the two friends held their breath as the driver walked past and climbed into the cab.

"Hey! Don! Gonna take folks riding on the balloon today?" another truck driver called out.

"Naw, Sam and I are just trying out a new basket. If it works, we'll be taking a bunch of Boy Scouts up tomorrow. Hope we get some nice weather!"

"The driver, Don, must be the Amazing Donald," Fool whispered to Intuit. As if in agreement, Intuit nuzzled his wet nose into Fool's neck.

Closing the door of his truck, Amazing Donald waved cheerfully to the other driver. Engines roaring, he drove out of the station toward the highway leading away from the city.

Lulled by the rumbling of the truck's big engine, Fool and Intuit fell asleep in the giant basket. Sleeping soundly, they didn't feel the truck rumble to a stop. They didn't even hear Amazing Donald and Sam slamming doors as they got out of the truck.

"Hey, who's sleeping in my basket?" Amazing Donald roared, lifting the folds of material. Fool and Intuit blinked sleepily in the morning sunlight. "What are you doing in there?"

"Oh, Mr. Amazing," stuttered Fool. "I'm sorry. It's just that we wanted to see the forest, and we hoped we could get a ride on your balloon over the forest, like..... like the sign on your truck said!"

"Sounds like you want a free ride, boy!" thundered Amazing Donald. "Nobody gets a free ride on *this* balloon! And besides, wait till your parents find out you hitched a ride all the way out to the country. They'll be worried to tears. And they'll probably be really miffed at me. Well, I guess I'll just have to take you back. But first, I have to test out this new basket. Tell you what, boy, you help Sam and me set up this balloon, and I'll give you and the dog here a little test ride over that forest you wanted to see. Then it's back to the city and to your parents!"

Sensing that everything was okay, Intuit began barking and dancing round and round in circles. Smiling with relief, Fool hurried to help the two men. Amazing Donald and his partner, Sam, showed Fool how to carry the ropes and how to unfold the material. It took almost all morning to set up the hot air balloon, but at last it was ready. The huge balloon was covered with red, yellow and blue stripes. As they worked, Sam explained how hot air balloons operate.

"You see, boy, to make a balloon, what we pros call an envelope, rise, the air inside the balloon has to be warmer than the outside air. To fill the balloon with hot air, we heat propane using this little outfit called a burner." Holding the burner for Fool to examine, he went on. "When the propane is ignited, it turns to hot vapor and fills the balloon." Pulling on a little valve, Amazing Donald opened the burner flame and ignited the propane.

WHOOSH! WHOOSH! Warm air began to fill the large, colorful balloon.

"How do you steer this thing?" asked Fool.

"Ride the wind, my boy!" laughed Amazing Donald. "Ride the wind! Just find an air current that's going your way. And then," he narrowed his eyes and looked directly at Fool, "you just hitch a ride!"

Blushing, Fool looked at the ground for a minute. "How do you land?"

"Here," said Amazing Donald, handing Fool a long, nylon cord. "When we're ready to land, we'll just pull on this cord. It opens a little hole in the top of the balloon and allows some of the air to escape. Then, we'll drift down slowly." As he talked, the balloon continued to fill with hot air. "Well, that's about it," he said, pulling the burner valve one more time. WHOOSH! The balloon, now full of hot vapor, tugged on the basket tied to the ground. "Now, you and I and that dog of yours will take a little ride. Sam here, will follow us on the ground in the truck. When we're ready to land, we'll head for the road and he can drive right up to us, and we can pack up and go home. Hop in. Sam will untie us and we're ready to fly!"

Climbing aboard, Fool shivered with goose bumps of excitement. Within moments, the balloon began to rise. Looking over the edge of the basket, it seemed to Fool that the ground was falling away! Rising slowly at first, then faster and faster, the balloon lifted until it was so high that Fool could see the tops of barns, houses, trees and roads! Looking like a very small toy, the truck below followed the path of the colorful balloon. An occasional WHOOSH! of the burner was the only sound high above the ground.

"Well," said Amazing Donald, "looks like this basket is going to work just fine!" Feeling less grumpy than when he'd found Fool and Intuit, Amazing Donald chatted cheerfully.

"We'll float around over the farm areas for awhile, then we'll take a swing over the forest. After that, it's back to flat land. Usually while we're up here, I like to tell a joke or two. The riders seem to enjoy it. I need some new ones, though. Say, kid, do you know any good jokes?"

Fool thought for awhile. "No," he answered, "but I do know a story. A story about flying, but not about flying in a balloon."

"A story!" laughed Amazing Donald. "Gee, its been a long time since anyone told me a story. Yeah, go for it. I could use a good story. But, first, let's get the balloon up higher. That way we won't need as much hot air, and we won't have to listen to the noise of the burner. We can talk in peace and quiet."

Catching a warm updraft, the balloon drifted higher over the countryside looking, from the ground, like a tiny, colorful butterfly playing tag with the clouds. As the balloon floated peacefully over the land, Amazing Donald settled back and relaxed. Fool began his story.

This is the story Fool shared with the Amazing Donald as they floated above the world in a red, yellow and blue balloon.

Chapter Four

Frequent Flyer

"Now, ladies and gentlemen, please return your seats and tray tables to their upright and locked positions and we'll be ready to fly! Flight attendants, please take your seats and prepare for take off." Captain Kenny's voice boomed pleasantly over the loud speaker.

Giving the cabin one last quick glance, Ms. Baker, the head flight attendant, smiled at Nancie, gave her a little wink, turned, and joined the other attendants in the special chairs designed for airline crew.

"This is it! Here we go again!" Nancie thought to herself, gripping the arm of her seat with her left hand and crossing the fingers on her right hand. Tightly shutting her eyes and holding her breath, she prepared to feel her stomach turn somersaults.

Each summer Nancie flew from Los Angeles, where her mother lived, to Cape Cod to spend time with her father. Although always happy to see her other parent, secretly, deep down inside, flying in airplanes frightened her. Sitting straight in her airline seat waiting for the big plane to move down the runway, Nancie thought back to when she first learned she would be taking these trips.

It happened two days after her fifth birthday. She could remember the feel of the sunshine on her cheeks and the soft wind blowing wisps of hair across her face as she walked through the L.A. zoo with her parents.

"Your mother and I love each other very much," her father began.

"And we both love you, dearly," her mother added quickly.

Her father continued, "When people love each other, they grow. Sometimes when they grow, they get more alike. Sometimes when they grow, they become more individual."

"Your father and I have been growing a great deal, Honey," her mother said, smiling softly at Nancie's father, "and, as we've grown, we've discovered that we like very different things."

"Except, of course, you!" laughed her father, picking Nancie off the ground and twirling her around in the air. "We both like you bunches." Giving her a little squeeze, he lowered her back to the ground.

"What kind of different things?" Nancie asked, looking up at her pretty mother.

Perfectly twisted into a braided knot, her mother's jet black hair glistened in the sunlight. Bending down to be eye level with her daughter, her perfume enveloped Nancie in a sweet, fresh cloud. "Things like where we want to live," she answered. "I want to live in Los Angeles in a big, modern apartment building. I want to ride a shiny elevator up eleven flights to my apartment! Your father wants to live in a little cottage on a beach. He wants to walk by the ocean everyday. I want to ride around the city in a taxi. Things like that."

Kneeling down to join Nancie and his wife, Nancie's father added, "And, we like different kinds of work. Your mom wants to practice interior decorating. She wants to help people pick out drapery and furniture for their homes. I want to be an artist. I want to use pieces of rock and wood and shells to make art that hangs from ceilings and dances in the wind. You know, Pumpkin, things like that!"

"Well, how can you do those different things?" Nancie asked, looking from parent to parent in confusion.

"Easy, Honey," her mother smiled. "I will live in Los Angeles, and your father will live in Cape Cod. You remember the Cape, don't you? Remember when we visited Grandma and Grandpa last summer?"

Nodding slowly, Nancie said, "Yes, I remember Cape Cod. It's nice. But... but, what about me? Where will I live?" she stuttered, warming up for a cry.

"Honey, that's the really great part." Reaching over and giving Nancie a big hug, her father smiled and explained. "You'll get to do both fun things. In the summer you get to run on the beach and help me collect shells and stones and things. You'll have wonderful friends to play with all summer long."

"Yes!" her mother interrupted eagerly, "and every fall you'll come back to Los Angeles and go to school with a whole new set of friends! You'll have the best of two, really fun, worlds!"

"Ladies and gentlemen, we're cleared for take off. Sit back and enjoy the ride!" Captain Kenny's voice crackled over the speaker, breaking into Nancie's memory. Moving slowly at first, then faster and faster, the big plane taxied down the runway.

For just a second, Nancie opened her eyes to look at the passengers sitting on either side of her. On her left side, a very fat man wearing a wrinkled business suit settled down for a snooze. His tie was pulled half off, twisted in a knot, and his belly peeked out of the buttons on his shirt. Snoring softly, he didn't even feel the moving plane.

On her right side, in the window seat, sat a tiny old woman. Skinny and small, she wore a peach dress with pink and purple flowers splashed over the fabric. Her ancient, black shoes had square heels, and her glasses were small circles held together by thin, gold wires. Several wispy strands of gray hair escaped from the little bun on top of her head, giving her the appearance of an old fashioned school teacher on a windy day. Sunk into her seat, her eyes tightly closed, she kept twisting and untwisting a white, lace hankie.

Forgetting her own fear of takeoffs for a moment, Nancie turned and watched the old woman. Feeling someone staring at her, the lady opened her eyes and tried her best to smile.

Nancie realized the frail, older woman felt like she did... scared, very scared. "Hi! My name is Nancie, are you going to Los Angeles, too?"

"Uh huh," the woman answered in a shaky, frightened voice. "Lord willing! I've never been in one of these contraptions, and I don't know. I just don't know." Her small blue eyes grew bigger and bigger while the rest of her shrank smaller and smaller into the seat.

"Oh," said Nancie. "This is your first time flying. Flying's always scary the first time. But my dad always says the *real* scary ride is driving home from the airport on the freeway!" The lady seemed confused. "It's just a joke. Daddy tells it every time, I mean *every* time we leave the airport." Still, the old woman didn't seem to get the joke.

Suddenly, picking up speed and tilting toward the sky, the plane raced along the runway. Grabbing the arms of her chair and gritting her teeth, the woman gasped. "Oh, my," she said, "I don't know if I like this at all. I just don't know."

"Don't worry about takeoffs," Nancie said seriously, suddenly feeling very experienced. "It's landing that's the hardest." Trembling, the old woman fought back tears. Immediately, Nancie wished she hadn't said anything about landing.

Reaching over and placing her small hand on the old woman's wrinkled one, Nancie whispered, "You'll be all right." Smiling faintly, the old woman let go of the arm of her chair and gripped Nancie's hand. Holding tightly to each other's hands, the two flyers squeezed their eyes shut and held their breath.

Shuddering once, with great engines roaring, the big, silver plane tilted upward more steeply, launching itself into the sky. Flipping over twice, Nancie's stomach told her they were airborne.

Captain Kenny's voice filled the cabin. "Well, folks, we had a pretty smooth takeoff! In just a few minutes we'll be reaching our cruising altitude. The flight attendants will be coming around with beverages, and in not too long we'll begin our inflight meal service. Just sit back and relax, folks, and leave the flying to us!"

"You can open your eyes now," Nancie offered, noticing that the old woman's eyes were still squeezed shut. "And, if you look out, you can see houses and cars on the ground!" she added enthusiastically.

"Oh, my, no!" whispered the woman, opening her eyes to peek at Nancie. "I don't want to look at the ground." Her voice shook and Nancie felt sure the frightened lady would soon be crying. She tried to think of everything that all the flight attendants and friendly people sitting next to her had ever said when she felt afraid.

"Well," she suggested, "pretty soon they'll bring around the sodas and peanuts. Then you'll feel better."

Lifting her crumpled hankie to her lips and trembling, the woman answered, "Oh! I can't eat anything. I'd just spill it or throw up."

Nancie decided not to say anything else about eating for awhile. Trying something different, she took a deep breath, and pretending to be calm and relaxed, she repeated, "My name is Nancie. I'm flying to Los Angeles to be with my mother, and to go to school. I'll be in the fifth grade this year." Noticing the woman relaxing just a bit, she went on, "It looks like this is your first time in an airplane. Why are you flying to Los Angeles?"

Turning in her chair to look at Nancie, the woman took a deep breath. "Well," she began shyly, "you're right. This is my first time flying. I guess it really shows! My name is Mabel. Mabel Thompson. I'm going to see a friend of mine... a fellow." The pale white of Mabel Thompson's face turned a soft pink.

"Oh!" said Nancie, "your boyfriend!"

"Well, I don't know about that." Mabel's pink cheeks flushed to a deep rose color. Sitting up a little straighter in her chair and letting go of the arm rest, she continued. "I met him this summer when he came to the Cape to visit his son." Talking about her friend, Mabel forgot her fear for a few minutes. "My husband died a long time ago, and I never went out with anyone else till this fellow came around. This fellow, well, he's really very special." Turning her face to hide her blush, Mabel glanced out the window for a second. Gasping, she turned back quickly.

Grabbing Mabel's hand and giving it a quick squeeze, Nancie encouraged her, "Go on. Tell me more about your fellow."

Mabel let out a deep breath and went on. Her face glowing, she spoke of planting flowers, visiting local museums, and of listening to records from the old days with her special friend. As she spoke her eyes sparkled and her voice grew steady.

Just as she began telling Nancie about a special dinner they'd shared, the plane shuddered and dipped. Nancie's stomach did another double flip.

"Folks, we're experiencing a bit of turbulence, so fasten your seat belts and stay in your seats for awhile. We'll be out of it soon," explained Captain Kenny over the speaker.

The color had drained from Mabel's face. Grabbing the chair arm and squeezing her eyes shut tight, she sank deep into her seat and stopped talking.

"Don't worry," Nancie said quickly. "This sort of thing happens all the time." But Mabel didn't hear a thing. She just sat motionless with fear. Feeling frustrated and a bit discouraged, Nancie let out a big sigh. "Geepers," she thought to herself, "I am a very experienced flyer. I ought to be able to help this lady feel better. There must be a way!"

As Nancie pondered the problem, Captain Kenny announced that the plane had traveled out of the rough weather and that anyone wanting to move about the cabin could do so freely.

"But, while you're in your seats," he reminded the passengers, "please make sure you wear your seatbelt at all times." Something about the captain's announcement reminded Nancie of her first time on an airplane. Getting an idea, she unfastened her seatbelt and stood up.

"You're not going to walk around, are you?" Mabel's terrified eyes snapped open.

Bending over, Nancie patted the old hand now glued to the chair handle. "Don't worry," she said, smiling. "I'll be perfectly okay!"

Acting brave for the sake of her fellow passenger, Nancie smiled as she stood. Moving around in airplanes frightened her more than any other part of flying. Slowly, and very carefully, she walked from one seat to the next, grabbing the back of each chair as she went. Holding tightly to the seatbacks, and looking straight ahead, Nancie didn't notice any of the people filling the crowded plane. Moving slowly, she progressed chair by chair down the aisle toward the rear.

Reaching the last row, she sighed with relief and leaned against the restroom door. Noticing her, a flight attendant said, "You can go in, Honey; no one's in there now." Pulling little trays of hot food from an oven and stacking them on a cart, the young woman smiled pleasantly at Nancie.

"Oh, I don't need to go. May I have a pair of those silver wings you give to little kids?" Nancie asked.

"Well, sure, hon," answered the attendant, adding another tray to the stack. "But I'm a little busy right now, can you wait for awhile?"

"Of course!" Nancie smiled gratefully, pleased to be able to delay the long walk back to her seat. "Thank you so much." Watching the attendant busy with her work, Nancie chatted about the wings.

"They're not for me," she explained. "They're for an old lady up in the front. This is her first airplane ride, and she's very scared. I thought maybe the wings would help her feel better."

Stopping her work, the flight attendant took a long look at Nancie.

"That's a very sweet thought," she said softly. Kneeling down she began poking around in a box stored under the last seat. "Why is the lady flying with us today?"

"She's doing something scary because she loves someone," Nancie answered solemnly. Stopping her search for a minute, the attendant took another long look at Nancie.

"And, why are you flying with us today?" she asked.

Looking down at her shoes, Nancie thought of her father running on the sandy beach of Cape Cod. And she thought of her beautiful mother smiling at the doorman as they entered the tall L.A. apartment building.

"I guess I'm doing it because I love someone, too," she answered quietly.

Smiling, the flight attendant stood up. "Here it is! Good Luck! Hope it helps!" she said, handing Nancie a small, silver pin shaped like two eagle wings.

Hurrying back to her seat, moving much faster than before, Nancie noticed several people smiling at her. Feeling quite confident, she smiled back.

"Made it!" she exclaimed, squeezing past the still sleeping businessman and climbing into her seat.

Eyeing Nancie, Mabel said, "You look pretty happy. What have you been up to?"

"Well," answered Nancie, grinning, "I know why you've felt so scared."

"You do?" Opening her eyes wide, Mabel sat up and stared at Nancie.

"Yes," nodded Nancie. "They forgot to give you your wings! That's the only problem!"

"What?" asked Mabel, clearly confused.

"They forgot to give you your wings," Nancie repeated, holding out the silver pin. "Here, let me help put them on you." Kneeling on the plane seat, Nancie leaned over and pinned the silver wings to the lace collar of Mabel's flowered dress.

"You see," she explained, "when you fly on a plane for the first time, you're supposed to get a pair of silver wings. The wings protect you. They help make new flyers safe. All kids get them. I guess they just forgot to give you your wings, 'cause, well, maybe they thought you've been on a plane before. But trust me, these wings will really make everything better!" Sitting back down in her seat, Nancie smiled up at Mabel. "You'll see. Now you'll start to feel better right away!"

"Well. My goodness," said Mabel. Taking a deep breath and sitting up a little straighter in her chair, she reached up and touched the wings. "I guess I do feel a little better."

"Good!" Nancie grinned. "And just in time for lunch!"

Carefully placing trays of food on the lowered tables in front of Nancie and Mabel, the flight attendant noticed the silver pin on Mabel's collar. Winking at Nancie she smiled. "Have a nice lunch, ladies!"

Enjoying their meal of green salad, creamed chicken, and brown sugar carrots, the two flyers shared stories about people they knew and loved.

"You should see the art Dad makes from stuff he finds on the beach!" Nancie giggled, remembering her father. "One time he made a really big thing out of feathers and shells. He hung it from the ceiling. I thought it looked like a big bird, so Dad started pretending he was a bird. He flapped his arms and jumped up and down on the bed. He jumped up so high he hit the hanging thing with his arm, and it came crashing down on his head!"

Watching Nancie imitate her father, Mabel burst out laughing. "Your father sounds like a wonderful man!" Mabel said, catching her breath.

"He is," Nancie agreed, nodding her head. "And, he's a real nut!"

"What about your mother, dear? Is she a 'nut,' too?"

"Oh, no. Mother's very calm. She's also an artist, but in a different sort of way."

Sipping her tea and feeling quite relaxed, Mabel asked, "What kind of art does your mother do?"

"She's amazing!" Nancie answered enthusiastically. "Mother can walk into a dark, old building and, just by decorating, she can figure out a way to make it look like... like," she hesitated, thinking of the right words, "like really rich people live there!"

"That is amazing," agreed Mabel, reaching up every few minutes to touch the silver wings. Feeling the cool metal, she sighed and breathed a little easier.

Nancie and Mabel continued chatting and laughing for several hours. Time slipped by. Captain Kenny's announcement of their arrival over California came as a surprise to both of them.

"O.K. folks, we made it! Fasten those seat belts and we'll be in Los Angeles in just a few minutes. Flight attendants, please prepare for landing."

Circling in wide, lazy rings, the airplane dropped slowly toward the busy airport.

Leaning over, Nancie whispered in Mabel's ear, "Don't worry about the landing business. You're wearing your wings now. It's really easy!"

Smiling, Mabel reached for Nancie's hand. Touching her pin with one hand and holding Nancie's hand tightly with the other, Mabel kept her eyes open during the entire descent. Once she even peeked out the window as the toy sized buildings and highways grew larger and larger.

Landing with a gentle thud, the plane rolled onto the runway.

"That's all folks!" laughed Captain Kenny over the speaker. "Now you'll be heading onto the Los Angeles freeway, and the really scary ride begins!" Nancie and Mabel looked at each other and laughed.

"Would you like to go to the gate with me and meet my gentleman friend?" Mabel asked.

"I'm sorry, I can't," Nancie replied. "Kids traveling alone have to wait for airline assistants to help them off planes. But say 'Hi!' for me! And," she added, "be sure to wear your wings when you fly back home!"

Reaching up and touching her pin, Mabel smiled at Nancie and disappeared into the crush of people crowding to get off the plane.

Arriving as soon as the last passenger left the plane, an airline assistant greeted Nancie.

"Hi, there! Hold on a second and I'll lift your bag down, and we'll go meet your mom!" Within minutes, Nancie and the pleasant assistant left the plane and headed into hot California sunshine. Happy to be getting closer to her mother, Nancie skipped along, smiling and chatting about the flight.

Sitting in the cockpit of the big plane, Captain Kenny watched as the last of his passengers walked toward the airport gate. Seeing Nancie and the airplane assistant, he shook his head, quickly looked away, then looked back again. Rubbing his eyes and turning to his copilot he said, "I really have to get some shuteye. I'm starting to see things." Shaking his head, he looked out the plane window once more. Skipping across the tarmac, Nancie looked just like a normal, little girl... except that fluttering lightly on her back were two large, shimmering, angel wings.

"Look at that kid," he said, turning to the flight attendant. "See anything unusual?"

"No," answered the attendant, peering out the cockpit window. "But I talked to her during the flight, and I can tell you, she's a little angel. She's a perfect frequent flyer!"

Nancie didn't see her new wings, and the airplane assistant didn't see them. As Nancie passed through the airport gate, her mother noticed a warm glow around her daughter. However, she didn't see the wings either. But they were there. And, although not many people can see them, Nancie still wears shining angel wings that glisten and shimmer in the bright, afternoon sun.

Fool's Journey

<u>Where Fool and Intuit sneak into the forest, and</u>
<u>Intuit prepares to do battle with an old brown bear.</u>

"Good story, kid!" said Amazing Donald when Fool had finished. "A little far fetched, I mean angel wings and all, but maybe the scouts will enjoy it. Mind if I pass it along?"

"Oh, no, not at all!" Fool answered. "The stories are meant to be shared... especially with children." As Fool began to ask Amazing Donald if he'd like to hear another story, the balloon turned toward the forest. Smelling the sweet fragrance of pine and fir trees drifting up into the air, Intuit started barking excitedly.

"Oh, look!" said Fool, staring down. "I love the forest!" Far below the tree tops looked like tiny, pointed green hats. Hundreds of them!

The sun traveled across the sky and the sweet moist smells of morning changed to powdered, dusty scents of afternoon. Drifting over perfect circles of low grass, Fool called out, "Look! Fairy rings!" Amazing Donald only grinned. Rivers and streams twisted and turned reminding Fool of Grandmother Hattie's long hair trailing over her shoulders and down the steps of her wooden porch. A family of deer raced the balloon's shadow across a daisy sprinkled meadow, then disappeared at the edge of a thick pine grove. Circling high above the balloon, a hawk cocked his head and wondered at the strange, bloated bird soaring below him.

As the balloon's shadow grew longer and longer across the forest floor, Amazing Donald began to seek air currents to ride back toward the flat land, to Sam and the truck. Fool shivered as the air began to cool. Dark rumbling clouds moved across the sky, slowly at first, then faster and faster. When the clouds were directly overhead, it started to rain.

"Darn," muttered Amazing Donald. "The rain made it before I planned." Turning to Fool he explained, "I really don't want to get this rig wet. I'm gonna set her down at the edge of the forest and get her back into the truck as soon as possible. There's a cover in the truck. It'll protect the basket from the rain."

Carefully and skillfully, Amazing Donald pulled the nylon cord and slowly released hot air, gently lowering the balloon to the ground. Moments later the balloon made a soft landing. Arriving soon after, Sam parked the truck and the two men quickly began deflating the balloon, winding ropes, unhitching the basket, and doing all the other things it took to pack up the hot air balloon. Busy at their work, they didn't pay attention to Fool and Intuit. Quickly, and very quietly, the two friends slipped into the thick, green forest and disappeared from view.

Fool knew all about moving around in forests, and very soon he and Intuit were deep into the underbrush where Amazing Donald and Sam would not be able to find them. Although Fool felt a bit of sadness at having to leave without saying good-bye, or thanks for the balloon ride, he didn't want to go back to the city, not for a long time anyway. So, with his staff held over one shoulder, he and Intuit continued to move deeper and deeper into the forest, stopping now and then to chat with squirrels and birds, and once with a soft-eyed doe who stood daintily in a patch of sunlight at the edge of a ring of pines. As they traveled, the rain stopped and the sun dropped closer and closer to the edge of the earth. The air grew cooler and the smell of night blooming flowers began to mingle with the fading scent of daytime.

With evening slipping into the forest, Fool's stomach reminded him that he hadn't eaten since the delicious stew dinner the night before. And, although Fool loved being in forests, he realized he had no idea where he was. Intuit, growing weary from running through the forest, began sitting down every few minutes, directly in front of Fool. After tripping over his friend for the third time, Fool decided to take a supper break.

"Berries!" he thought. "I'll find some berries! There must be some ripe ones nearby." Watching the edge of the path more carefully now, urged on by his grumbling stomach, it didn't take much time to find the most luscious berry patch he had ever seen. Billions of dark, thick berries hung heavy on leafy bushes. Quickly, Fool started picking fat, round berries and popping them into his mouth, making sure to offer handfuls to Intuit as well. Just as the berries began to fill his rumbling belly, Fool heard a tremendous roar.

"Who's eating my berries? GROWL!!! These are MY berries!!!" Frightened by the noise, Fool jumped back and dropped his handful of fruit. Intuit squealed and ran in the opposite direction down the path. Lumbering out from behind the bushes was the biggest, most ferocious bear in the whole world! At least the biggest, most ferocious bear in Fool's world!

"GROWL!!!!"

"Oh! Oh! Oh!" Fool stuttered.

"GROWL!" the bear bellowed again. "Is that all you can say, 'Oh! Oh! Oh!'? You're a berry thief, and now I'll have to eat **you** for dinner!"

Taking a big swipe with his mighty paw, the bear knocked leaves and berries all over the clearing, just missing Fool. Raising his paw to strike again, the bear roared loudly, shaking the entire forest.

"GROWL!!!"

Seeing his best friend in trouble, Intuit turned around and ran back, prepared to do battle with the giant bear.

"Ark, ark ark!" Intuit bristled, his fluffy fur giving him the appearance of being three times his real size.

The bear was so surprised that he stopped swinging for a moment and stared at the dog. Intuit, who normally looked merely like a silly, fluffy dog, was growling and barking and doing his very best to look extremely fierce.

Over all the noise Fool managed to yell out, "We're not berry thieves. I can pay for our dinner!"

"Pay for dinner?" The bear lowered his paw. Towering above them, the shaggy giant squinted suspiciously at the two berry patch intruders.

Standing his ground, Intuit continued a low growl.

"How can you pay for dinner? I'm a bear. I've no need for money! Do you have fat, juicy acorns for me to eat?"

"No," said Fool, "but, if you'll let us finish eating some of these delicious berries, Mr. Bear, I'll tell you a wonderful story. And you can tell the story to your bear cubs some day, or to your grand bear cubs."

At the mention of a story, the bear calmed down a bit. "Well, why didn't you say so earlier! I love stories. I've heard all the stories the squirrels tell, about a hundred times at least. I'd love to hear a new one. C'mon, little fellow, be my guest to these berries. Help yourself! And give some more to your little... uh... whatever this creature is."

So Intuit and Fool enjoyed a scrumptious dinner with their new found friend, the bear. After dinner, they all settled back against the rough bark of tall pine trees. Sliding from behind dark clouds, the shiny moon washed the forest with silver. Several small animals crept close to listen as Fool began his story. This is the story that Fool told the old bear in exchange for a dinner of berries.

Chapter Five

Sacred Circle

"Thanks, honey," said Michael's mother, smiling as he handed her the last of the dishes from the packing crate. "The kitchen is almost unpacked. I can take it from here. Why don't you two go out to the garage and see if your father needs any help?"

"O.K., Mom," Michael answered, heading out the kitchen door. "C'mon, Sarah, I'll race you across the yard!"

"No fair, you have a head start!" Pretending to complain, Sarah happily joined her brother in his dash out the door and across the yard. They were both excited because they were finally living in their first, very own, 'new house'. While new to the Daily family, the house was actually quite an antique. Older people, living in the surrounding areas, could remember the house standing there since their childhoods.

Dreaming of owning and fixing up an old farm house, the Dailys had worked extra jobs, skipped vacations, and saved their earnings. After spending a great deal of time, effort, and money, the family had transformed the beautiful house into a home. At last, the dream had become reality!

Standing alone on several acres of country land, the rambling estate looked especially inviting in the summer sunshine. Set back from the road at the end of a long driveway, it welcomed visitors with new white paint and slate blue trim. Standing three stories high, with gables and a peaked roof, the Daily house impressed all who viewed it. Surrounding the house on three sides, a wide wooden porch offered a great place for dreamy afternoons spent curled in one of several inviting wicker rocking chairs. A narrow railing ran all around the porch. Deep blue morning-glories twisted around two round pillars on either side of the front door. Hanging from the ceiling of the porch, new wicker baskets of coral geraniums, multi-colored pansies, and pink impatiens swayed and bobbed gracefully in the gentle breeze.

Inside the bright and sunny house, freshly polished hardwood covered all the floors. Large windows and tall ceilings gave the house a feeling of light and space. In a far corner of the huge back yard, a dilapidated chicken coop leaned to one side. An abandoned tool shed shared the opposite corner of the property with a boarded up outhouse.

Mr. Daily was especially proud of the only brand new structure on the property. He and two friends had spent several weekends building a three space garage in a sunny area behind the house. Two of the three spaces provided protection for the family cars. The third space served as storage and as a wood working shop for Mr. Daily.

"I won!" yelled Michael, rushing to touch the corner of the garage.

"I'll win next time!" panted Sarah, catching up with her brother. Following him through the little back door of the garage, she found her father busily unpacking. "Hi, Dad!"

"Hi, you two," her father replied. "You guys are just in time to help me stack these boxes of Christmas decorations. I think we'll put them over here behind my work benches. Be careful you don't drop any!"

Working with their father in the garage, Michael and Sarah forgot the time until Mrs. Daily called them in to dinner. After dinner, Sarah and her mother cleared the dishes, and Mr. Daily and Michael washed them and put them away. Exhausted from moving and unpacking, the Dailys headed to bed early.

"Sweet dreams, kids!" Mrs. Daily called, passing Michael's and Sarah's rooms on her way to bed. "Sleep well! We have a lot more unpacking to do tomorrow!" Night blooming jasmine filled the air with sweet fragrance, and soon the tired family snoozed peacefully in their beds, comfortably surrounded by their new, very own, home.

"CRASH! SLAM!"

Sitting straight up in her bed, Sarah glanced at the glowing clock on her radio - 2 AM. Listening carefully in the dark for more noise, she grabbed her bathrobe, slipped out of bed, and tiptoed into her brother's room across the hall. Hiding under the covers, with only his head peeking out, Michael shivered visibly.

"Did you hear that?" Sarah whispered.

"Yea!" he answered, pulling down the covers and sitting up. "What was it?"

"I don't know. It sounded like it came from the garage. Wanna go look?" she asked.

"Are you kidding? No way! I'm staying under the covers 'til daylight!"

"You chicken!" Sarah teased, punching her brother lightly on the arm. "I guess I'll wait until morning, too. Good night," she whispered, sneaking quietly back to her own room.

"Did you kids hear a noise coming from the garage last night?" Mr. Daily asked over breakfast the next morning. "Your mother and I thought we heard some crashing around in there."

"Yes!" they chimed in unison. "Let's go look!"

"Not until you finish your breakfast. We have a lot of unpacking to do this weekend, and I want you guys to stay healthy!" Mrs. Daily said, pretending to be stern.

Quickly finishing his eggs and winking at the children, Mr. Daily swallowed a final drop of coffee, eager himself to get out to the garage. Gulping down the last of their meals, Michael and Sarah joined their father as he sauntered into the bright morning sunshine en route to the garage.

"Well, would you look at this!" exclaimed Mr. Daily. Covering the concrete floor of the wood working area, tools of all shapes and sizes lay scattered about. A large tool box lay on its side, empty.

"I don't remember sitting this box so close to the edge. I don't understand how it could have fallen," mused Mr. Daily, scratching his head.

"Well, no real harm," he said, bending over to pick up the tools. "You kids go in and tell your mother everything is all right... and give her some help putting things away in the living room."

Working together, the Dailys rapidly completed unpacking and arranging their belongings. By the end of the first week of summer vacation, the family felt at home and comfortable in their new surroundings.

"I like everything about this place!" declared Mr. Daily at dinner one evening. "Except all that strange racket coming from the garage at night!"

"Well, I'm not especially fond of cleaning up the mess every morning, either," added Mrs. Daily. Sarah and Michael vigorously nodded their agreement. Around two o'clock, every night, sounds of crashing woke them up. And every morning after breakfast they encountered a new form of destruction in the garage.

One morning Mrs. Daily found her car door open. Another day, wood shavings littered the tops of both cars. After a night of particularly loud crashing, Sarah and Michael discovered that a whole box of light bulbs had fallen off a shelf. Landing on the cement floor, all but one of the bulbs were smashed to bits. Finally, an entire box of Christmas decorations, the ones Sarah and Michael had carefully stacked their first day of moving, tumbled to the floor, breaking most of the ornaments.

"This is ridiculous," Mr. Daily told his family. "There must be a large raccoon out in the garage. It's the only animal I can think of that would play those kinds of pranks! Tomorrow I'm going into town to the hardware store. I'll buy a wire trap, catch the raccoon without hurting him, and take him safely back to the forest where he belongs!"

That night, Michael and Sarah decided to sneak out to the garage to watch the raccoon before their dad trapped it and took it back to the woods. Shivering in the cool night air, Sarah sprinted across the lawn with her brother. The rich green grass was smooth and slidy. A heavy, round moon, spilling over with light, lit the way across the yard to the garage.

Quietly, Michael opened the small door that led to the wood working section. Holding one finger to his lips, he motioned to Sarah to be quiet as they snuck into the building. Sitting silently on the bench next to their father's work table, Sarah set her alarm watch for 2 AM. As she and Michael waited for the pesky raccoon to show it's furry face, the moon rose higher in the sky, shining through the window and changing the shadow patterns creeping across the garage. Leaning her head against her brother's shoulder, Sarah yawned, and fell gently into sleep. As she slept, the moon rose to it's peak, then dropped low in the sky, draping the garage in deep violet shadows.

"Beep beep! Beep beep!"

Waking with a start, Sarah realized that both she and Michael had fallen asleep. Her wrist watch was beeping out 2 AM. Sitting up straight she began to say something to Michael when she was suddenly stopped by a loud "CRASH!" A round, straw basket full of gardening tools tumbled off the edge of a shelf, spilling the tools all over the floor as it fell. Something, or someone, moved near the scattered tools. Michael grabbed Sarah's hand and gave a little squeeze.

"Is it the raccoon?" Sarah asked quietly.

"Shhh," Michael answered, holding his mouth close to her ear. Squinting her eyes, Sarah struggled to see in the darkened room.

"Wow!" whispered Michael, pointing across the wood shop. "That doesn't look like a raccoon to me!"

"Oh!" gasped Sarah, following her brother's finger with her eyes. Floating slowly above the scattered tools, a slender, young Indian girl, about 10 or 11 years old, shimmered in the fading moonlight. The fringe on her buckskin dress hung to her knees, swishing softly as she moved. Red and white beads sewn into the hide outlined designs of forests, flowers and streams. Looking almost wet, her shiny black hair, twisted into two long braids, trailed down her back. Not noticing Michael or his sister, she wandered around the woodshop appearing lost and confused. Finally, sitting down on the concrete floor of the garage, the girl began to cry.

Michael nudged his sister. "I can see right through her. Can you?" he whispered very softly, never taking his eyes off the Indian girl.

"Yes," his sister replied. "Weird, isn't it?"

"Weird is right." Michael whispered back. "She's a ghost and we should get out of here!" he said without moving.

"I don't care if she is a ghost." Sarah whispered, a little louder. "She's lost, or sad, or something, and I'm going to try and help, "she said, standing up.

"Are you crazy?" Michael whispered, grabbing at his sister's sleeve to pull her back to the bench.

It was too late. The Indian girl stopped sniffling and looked up.

"Ho!" she said, startled by the two children.

The children and the young Indian stared at each other for a full minute. Sarah swallowed hard and then, in as friendly a tone as she could manage, she squeaked, "Hello, my name is Sarah. This is my brother Michael. We just moved into the house next to this garage. What's your name?"

Looking rather surprised, the Indian answered, "My name is New Blossom. I live... I *used* to live on this land that is now your home." Again the Indian maiden and the children just stared at each other. "I'd better go," New Blossom said, beginning to fade around the edges.

"No!" shouted Michael, forgetting to be afraid. "I mean, stay! Tell us why you are unhappy."

The outline of New Blossom slowly strengthened. "Well," she began, "as you can probably see, I am in spirit. When I lived on the land that is now your home, it was my job to drum during rituals at the sacred medicine wheel circle. Now I am unhappy because the sacred circle is under all these heavy boxes, and this very hard, cold floor. Every night I come here to dance around the wheel and to drum at the sacred circle. When I cannot find the circle, I get sad, and mad, and confused, and I move things around, looking for what is lost."

Glancing first at her brother, then to New Blossom, Sarah cleared her throat and stuttered. "I... er, we didn't know. Dad, for sure, didn't know about the sacred medicine wheel. He wouldn't have put the garage here if he knew."

"She's right," added Michael. "We're sorry. It was a mistake. Is there anything we can do?"

"Can you help me find the sacred circle?" New Blossom pleaded.

"I don't know," Sarah answered. "But we can sure try. Give us a few days to figure out what we can do to help you. While we're doing that, please don't knock over any more things in the garage. Dad thinks you're a raccoon, and he's gonna set a trap for you!"

For the first time, New Blossom smiled. "I'm not concerned about your father," she grinned. "Spirits can't be captured... at least not in raccoon traps! But, I will honor your request." Promising to meet with the children on the next full moon, New Blossom faded slowly from view, leaving only the smell of flowers in the air.

Hurrying across the damp grass to the house, Michael and Sarah wondered about their experience. "Wow, were we dreaming or what?" Michael asked his sister.

"No, silly. If we were dreaming we wouldn't both see the same thing, would we?"

"Well, I guess not," said Michael nervously.

"And look, our shoes are wet from running across the grass!" Sarah pointed out. "No, she's a ghost all right, and we have to help her find that sacred circle!"

"You're probably right," agreed Michael as they snuck back into the house and climbed up the stairs to their bedrooms. "If we don't, she's going to cause lots of trouble out in Dad's woodshop!"

Entering her own room, Sarah whispered a final word to her brother. "Get some sleep, we'll figure something out!"

Thinking about New Blossom, the children fell asleep and dreamed of Indians, sacred drums and furry raccoons.

"You kids want to ride into town with me?" their father asked at breakfast the next morning. "I'm heading to the hardware store to get that raccoon trap."

Looking across the table at Sarah, Michael began to tell his father about the ghost. "Ah, Dad," he started, quickly stopping as Sarah kicked him under the table.

"What, son?" asked Mr. Daily looking over his coffee cup.

"Sure!" gulped Michael. "We'd love to ride into town with you!"

After breakfast the three headed out to the garage. Arriving at the scene of the latest mess, Mr. Daily shook his head and got into the car. As they climbed into the back seat of the car, Sarah and Michael could hardly keep from telling their father about the ghost. Grumbling about the overturned basket of garden tools, Mr. Daily backed the car out of the garage and headed into town.

"Here you go, mister," said Mr. Pennyworth, the old man who owned the hardware store. Handing a large trap to Mr. Daily, he offered, "You know, its none of my business. But you folks are new to the area and I think you ought to know."

"Know what?" asked Mr. Daily, taking money out of his wallet to pay for the trap.

"Well, I don't think you have a raccoon in there. That garage is built on some old Indian ground. What you probably have is a ghost." Michael and Sarah stopped looking at seeds and gardening tools, spun around, and stared at the shopkeeper.

"Don't be giving these kids any crazy ideas!" laughed Mr. Daily, picking up the trap and starting toward the door. "I'm pretty sure our little ghost will turn out to be furry, and very mischievous. Once he's back in the woods, the 'haunting' will stop! Bye now!"

Arriving home just before lunch, Michael and Sarah hurried upstairs to Sarah's room to talk. Whispering excitedly, they agreed,

"We've got to get back to Mr. Pennyworth and find out what he knows about our ghost!"

Two weeks later, Mr. Daily needed to go back to the hardware store for more supplies. Michael and Sarah begged a ride, and when they arrived, Michael distracted their father while Sarah talked to the owner.

"Mr. Pennyworth, remember what you said about our land being, well, haunted?"

"Sure do!" smiled Mr. Pennyworth, stamping prices on cardboard boxes of nails.

"I bet you've got an Indian ghost over there. My daddy used to tell me all about the Indians in this area. He knew one of the last ones to live around here. A woman by the name of Blossom, or Flower, or something like that. Mama died when I was born, and I guess the Indian helped Dad take care of me. I went to the city to live with relatives when I started school, so I don't remember much about her. After school, I went off to join the Army, and when I came back, she had died. All I can remember is that Dad was real fond of her. They spent many hours sitting on the bench in front of the store just talking and talking. Swapping stories, I guess."

"That's her!" exclaimed Sarah excitedly. "But she's a ghost now, and she looks like a girl about my age! She's upset because Dad's garage is built on top of her sacred circle ground. Is there anything we can do to help her?"

"Hmmmm," said Mr. Pennyworth, thoughtfully stroking his scruffy gray beard. "Well, I never really believed those stories, but then again, my daddy usually knew what he was talking about! Maybe you do have a ghost over there!"

"How can we help her?" Sarah pleaded with the shop owner. "Did your father tell you anything about medicine wheels or sacred circles?"

"No, not that I recall. But, I 'spec we can find out something about them," mused Mr. Pennyworth. "The thing is, we probably can't get your father to tear down that building. That three car garage cost a pretty nickel. Yep. But maybe you could make a medicine wheel somewhere close to the garage or something."

"But how? Dad will think we're nuts, and Mother wants to use the sunny patch behind the garage for a flower garden."

Pulling on his beard, Mr. Pennyworth thought for awhile. "Tell you what," he said, "maybe you could plant a flower garden in the shape of a medicine wheel. That way, your mother could have her flowers, and your ghost could have her circle, and your father's workshop will stay in one piece!"

Just then Mr. Daily walked over, interrupting the conversation. "This is it, I think," he said, putting a bunch of tools and supplies on the counter. "Can you think of anything else?" he asked, turning toward Sarah and Michael.

"Well, you know," Sarah began, "Mom wants a flower garden, and I was just thinking that planting one for her would be a nice summer project for Michael and me. We could put it in that sunny spot right behind the garage. It would be sort of a present for Mom!"

Michael glared at his sister. The last thing he wanted to do was plant a bunch of flowers during his summer vacation. Sarah winked, letting him know something was up.

"What a nice thought, Sarah-girl!" Her dad said, leaning down to give his daughter a big hug. "Tell you what, I'm going next door to get a haircut. Why don't you kids get Mr. Pennyworth here to help you pick out some bedding plants which will grow well in this area. You can surprise your mother when we get home."

Turning to Mr. Pennyworth he said, "Just ring up the kid's stuff with these other supplies, and I'll pay for all of it after my hair cut."

"Hot diggity!" said Mr. Pennyworth, slapping his bony knee after Mr. Daily left the store. "It worked!"

"What worked?" asked Michael, clearly confused.

"You tell your brother the plan," Mr. Pennyworth said, motioning to Sarah. "I'm going to the back room to see if I can find Dad's book on Indian lore." While the old man rummaged around in the back room, Sarah explained the plan to Michael.

"We can use this as a guide," said Mr. Pennyworth, returning with a worn, brown book covered with dust. "I knew I had something about Indians back there."

Pouring over the book the three conspirators found a picture of a medicine wheel along with a description of sacred circle ceremonies. "According to this book," said Mr. Pennyworth, skimming through the yellowed pages, "medicine wheels served as sacred circles, places to show respect to the forces of nature and the Great Spirit. Outlining sacred circles with rocks or even cornmeal, Indians honored all four directions, north, south, west and east. To show their reverence for the spirits of the elements, earth, air, water and fire, the Indians placed sacred objects in each section of the circle. They used rocks, feathers, shells filled with water, and flints. Drumming sacred dances they invited Spirits to participate in ceremonies of healing, spiritual communication, and growth."

"Wow," said Michael softly. "That's a lot of stuff to try to show in one little flower garden." Scrunching up his face and looking from Mr. Pennyworth to his sister, he asked, "How can we do it?"

"That's a very good question, son," Mr. Pennyworth replied, tugging on his beard.

"I know!" Sarah jumped up and began pacing back and forth excitedly. "We can represent the elements and the directions with color!"

"Color?" asked Michael doubtfully. "How?"

"Well, let's say each direction represents a different element," Sarah began.

"Says here, they do," interrupted Mr. Pennyworth, having turned several more pages as the children talked. "Based on the book, north is earth. The colors for earth are brown, black and dark green."

"Oh! I get it!" chimed in Michael. "South is hot, so it must represent fire. It must be red!"

"Right you are, son!" Beaming, Mr. Pennyworth went on. "East stands for air. Its colors are white and light violet."

"That leaves west, which has to be water," added Sarah happily. "And that means..."

Blue, they all called out at the same time! Laughing, the three friends began selecting plants that would work for the wheel, and for their mother's garden.

When their father returned, he found Sarah and Michael happily chatting with their new friend, Mr. Pennyworth. Joining his tools and the other supplies, a dozen small containers of young potting plants crowded the counter.

"Say," Mr. Pennyworth began as he rang up the order, "my grandkids live a long way from here. Don't get to see them much. I'd sure like to spend some time with these youngsters. My assistant can easily run the store for a few days. Maybe I could lend a hand on this garden stuff. Besides, my old bones could use a good workout in the sunshine!"

"Great!" grinned Mr. Daily. "You know the address. Why don't you stop by tomorrow morning around ten, and the three of you can get started!"

Arriving right on time, Mr. Pennyworth joined Michael and Sarah behind the garage. After an hour of careful planning, the three friends began to work the rich, warm soil, preparing the earth for a colorful, living, sacred medicine wheel.

Each day for a whole week, Mr. Pennyworth drove to the Daily's home in the country. Joining Michael and Sarah he dug, planted, and watered. Using string tied to small stakes, they outlined the four different directions. Carefully choosing flowers that would grow in colors to represent the elements, they nurtured the small plants.

Continuing their nurturing by watering and weeding each day, the children and Mr. Pennyworth felt their anticipation increase as the little plants grew taller and stronger. The day before the next full moon, Sarah remembered New Blossom's promise to visit them. She asked Mr. Pennyworth to drive out to the house late at night to greet the Indian maiden.

"I'd love to meet her," said Mr. Pennyworth. "But, I don't see well enough to drive at night. You'll just have to say 'Hello' for me."

"There must be a way!" Michael said, shaking his head. "You've done all this work, and the garden is almost ready to blossom. She'll want to thank you!"

"Oh, there you are, hard at work in the garden again!" Walking round the corner of the garage, Mrs. Daily smiled at the three gardeners. Setting down a large plate of chocolate chip cookies and a pitcher of lemonade, she said, "Here's a treat. Take a break. Your little plants look very healthy! I can hardly wait to see your circle bloom! I'm sure it will be very special!"

"Very special, Mom!" said Michael, winking at Sarah and reaching for a cookie.

Turning to the oldest gardener, Mrs. Daily said, "Mr. Pennyworth, the children's father and I have a favor to ask of you. We need to drive to the city tomorrow on some business, and we'd like to spend the night there. Would you mind watching the children for us? You can use our guest bedroom, and the kids can cook you a nice dinner. What do you say?"

The three gardeners stopped munching cookies and stared at Mrs. Daily. This was the very thing they needed! Gaining his composure and clearing his throat, Mr. Pennyworth stammered, "Thank you, Mrs. Daily. I'd be happy to mind the children tomorrow evening!"

"Good! It's settled then!" Smiling, she turned and strolled back across the lawn to the house.

The next night, after their parents were gone, and when the dinner dishes were washed and put away, Sarah, Michael, and Mr. Pennyworth all went to their rooms for a short rest before waking to meet New Blossom. At 1:30 AM, three alarm clocks jangled loudly.

"Hurry!" called Sarah, pulling on a warm sweater as she scrambled down the stairs and out the back door. Catching up with her, Mr. Pennyworth and Michael hustled across the lawn to the new, freshly planted garden. Sitting quietly, next to the garden, the three waited for 2 AM, New Blossom's arrival time.

"Beep beep! Beep beep!" Sarah's watch announced the hour.

Shivering in the moonlight, Michael whispered, "She should be here soon!"

At that very moment a shimmering mist formed in the center of the garden. Slowly at first, then faster and faster, the mist became thicker and thicker, taking the form of New Blossom. Floating over the garden, she smiled at Michael, Sarah, and Mr. Pennyworth.

"So this is the sacred circle!" she said. "I know it is going to be beautiful! You are so kind to help me this way." Looking directly at Mr. Pennyworth, she asked, "Old friend, can you see me?"

"Of course," he answered, softly. "You are the Indian woman my father talked about! You are so beautiful."

"Thank you," she replied. "Your father and I were very close in life, and," she added, smiling wistfully, "we are still close in spirit."

Sarah and Michael looked at each other in amazement. While they watched a young Indian girl float lightly in the night mists, Mr. Pennyworth obviously talked with a grown up Indian woman!

"Is the wheel correct?" asked Mr. Pennyworth, hopefully. "Can you perform your ceremonies here?"

"Oh, yes, dear friend," she answered gently. "But the wheel needs just one more thing. Something I gave to your father long ago will complete the sacred circle."

"What? What is it?" asked Mr. Pennyworth, quizzically.

Gently, New Blossom explained. "In the center of a sacred medicine wheel, sits an altar. This is a special place of honoring Spirit. It may be a bowl for burning sage, or a basket of flowers. In the back of your shop, in a corner under the attic stairs, sits an old, handmade Indian pot. Put it in the center of the circle. Plant something in it to remind you of the spirit of the Indians, and," she added softly, "something to remind you of the spirit of your wonderful father."

Turning to Michael and Sarah, New Blossom smiled. "Thank you so much for helping me to find the sacred circle. Now, I will drum for you." As she spoke, an Indian drum painted with scenes of valleys, forests, flowers, and animals appeared in New Blossom's hands. She began drumming slowly and softly. Gradually, the drumming became louder and stronger. Called by the sacred music, misty shapes began to emerge around New Blossom. One by one, the spirits of Indians, old and young, floated over the sacred circle. Toe, heel, toe, heel, the spirits tapped out dances honoring the elements of nature and the Great Spirit. Watching the shimmering spirits in sacred ceremony, Sarah, Michael, and Mr. Pennyworth felt their hearts fill with great peace and love.

Slowly the sound of drumming softened. As the music faded, the spirits of the Indians faded as well, until only New Blossom's image remained. Looking up from her drum, she smiled once more at Mr. Pennyworth and the two children, and then very gently, she too, faded from view.

The night grew still and very, very quiet. Standing up, without saying a word, the three friends walked silently back to the house, and to their own rooms. Nobody felt much like talking.

Throughout the remainder of the summer, Mr. Pennyworth, Sarah and Michael gathered together nearly every morning to weed, water and encourage the little plants. Soon the garden was bursting with color. Standing by the circle on a late August afternoon, they surveyed their work.

Divided into four sections, the wheel, splashed with color, sent clouds of sweet fragrance into the warm breeze. To the south, fiery red and orange Indian paintbrush blooms tossed and bounced in the wind. To the west, slender bluebell flowers swayed gracefully. Crowds of bright, white daisies pointed east, and deep green sage covered the earth of the north. Sitting directly in the center of the wheel, honoring the spirits of an Indian woman and an old shopkeeper, a worn, terra cotta pot mixed the deep gold color of black-eyed Susans with the cheerful periwinkle blue of bachelor buttons.

"Well, kids, I think we really did it!" Mr. Pennyworth said, with awe and wonder. "I think this really is a very sacred circle!"

"What a great summer!" said Michael. "I can't believe its almost time to go back to school."

"Yes," his sister added. "I wonder if our teachers will understand our reports on what we did over summer vacation!" Laughing together, the three friends turned and walked toward the house for lunch.

New Blossom didn't return. At least she didn't show herself to the children, or to anyone else. But every summer, on the night of each full moon, the soft sound of Indian drumming can be heard drifting on the summer breezes. And the sound always seems to come from a very special circle of summer flowers.

Fool's Journey

<u>Where Fool is just too tired to go on, and
the old brown bear finds a simple solution.</u>

Fool, Intuit and the bear spent all summer and late into the fall wandering the woods, eating berries and acorns and swapping stories. Squirrels, birds, rabbits, deer and other animals listened in, chuckling and clapping at the funny parts and huddling together during the scary parts. The happy, healthy friends spent so much time playing and enjoying life, they hardly noticed the forest, and the seasons, changing.

The days grew shorter and shorter, and the nights became colder and colder, until one morning Fool woke feeling stiff and very uncomfortable. Seeing his breath in the snappy morning air, he realized his summer adventure would soon come to a close.

"I'm very fond of the forest, the bear and all the other animals," he mumbled to himself. "But, I miss the children. It's been a long time since I've visited the magical cottage of Grandmother Hattie. And," he added, stomping his feet to warm them, "I don't ever remember the Land of Dreams being this cold!"

Feeling depressed, Fool leaned on his staff and complained to the bear. "Bear," he grumbled, "it's getting too cold to wander the forest. I don't have a thick, fur coat, like you. What will we do when the snow starts falling?"

"Don't worry," answered the bear. "Every winter I move into a nice, dry cave. It's not too far from here. I guess it's about time to head that way now. Follow me." Lumbering along, the bear led Fool and Intuit up the side of a small cliff. At the top he stopped. Pushing away one branch of a ragged fir tree and revealing the door of a cozy little cave, he announced, "Welcome, friends, to my winter home!"

Barking joyfully, Intuit bounced past the bear and began sniffing every inch of the cave. Following close behind, Fool and the bear entered through the small opening, letting the fir branch fall back into place behind them.

"See," the bear pointed out to Fool, "the tree branch is just like a curtain over a window! We can see out, but passers-by can't see in. I like my privacy in the winter!"

Looking out the door of the cave, Fool watched fluffy white snowflakes begin to drift from thick gray clouds.

"Ahh gee..." Fool sighed a long, weary sigh. "I'm so tired, I feel like I can't go on. So many things have happened. I just feel exhausted. I've been so busy. And, I miss the Land of Dreams and my friends back home. I just don't know what to do." Staring out at the big fluffy flakes of snow, he sighed again.

"Well, I don't know about you," grumbled the old bear, "but whenever I get feeling that way... you know, tired... completely down... not knowing what to do, well, what I do is, I take a nap. A long, restful nap."

"You're so silly!" snapped Fool. "You're a bear! Every winter *all* bears go to sleep for the entire season. It's not a nap, it's called hibernation! You just simply go into hibernation!"

Grumbling softly to himself, the old bear slowly turned round and round making a nest of the grass and dried leaves on the floor of the cave. He plopped down comfortably, causing little puffs of dust to pouf up from under his heavy winter coat. Yawning a big, slow yawn he stretched out his shaggy legs.

"Call it what you will," he mumbled, lowering his chin to his paw, "but I call it a nap."

Seeing a good opportunity, Intuit immediately trotted over to where the bear was resting. Curling around three times into a doggy sized nest, he flopped down right next to the belly of the old brown bear.

Pushing his nose deep into the bear's warm tummy, he was soon snoring. Paws twitching slightly, Intuit began to dream of butterflies and squirrels, boat rides and happy, happy mornings.

"Ahhhhh," sighed Fool, gazing out again at the quickly deepening winter. He looked at his two friends slumbering peacefully in their nests of dried grass and leaves. Turning, he stared once more out of the cave. Watching the forest change from bright greens and browns to quiet blue-grays, he sighed again. With a soft smile Fool left the door of the cave, propped his staff safely against a wall, and walked over to his sleeping friends. He knelt down and stroked the scraggly fur of the old bear. Then he leaned over and gently kissed the top of Intuit's fluffy yellow head. Sighing again, Fool curled up next to Intuit in the warmth of the bear's soft belly. Snuggling together in the warm, dry cave, and dreaming sweet dreams, the three friends drifted into long and peaceful naps.